The Companions of the Ace High by Edgar Wallace

Richard Horatio Edgar Wallace was born on the 1st April 1875 in Greenwich, London. Leaving school at 12 because of truancy, by the age of fifteen he had experience; selling newspapers, as a worker in a rubber factory, as a shoe shop assistant, as a milk delivery boy and as a ship's cook.

By 1894 he was engaged but broke it off to join the Infantry being posted to South Africa. He also changed his name to Edgar Wallace which he took from Lew Wallace, the author of Ben-Hur.

In Cape Town in 1898 he met Rudyard Kipling and was inspired to begin writing. His first collection of ballads, The Mission that Failed! was enough of a success that in 1899 he paid his way out of the armed forces in order to turn to writing full time.

By 1904 he had completed his first thriller, The Four Just Men. Since nobody would publish it he resorted to setting up his own publishing company which he called Tallis Press.

In 1911 his Congolese stories were published in a collection called Sanders of the River, which became a bestseller. He also started his own racing papers, Bibury's and R. E. Walton's Weekly, eventually buying his own racehorses and losing thousands gambling. A life of exceptionally high income was also mirrored with exceptionally large spending and debts.

Wallace now began to take his career as a fiction writer more seriously, signing with Hodder and Stoughton in 1921. He was marketed as the 'King of Thrillers' and they gave him the trademark image of a trilby, a cigarette holder and a yellow Rolls Royce. He was truly prolific, capable not only of producing a 70,000 word novel in three days but of doing three novels in a row in such a manner. It was estimated that by 1928 one in four books being read was written by Wallace, for alongside his famous thrillers he wrote variously in other genres, including science fiction, non-fiction accounts of WWI which amounted to ten volumes and screen plays. Eventually he would reach the remarkable total of 170 novels, 18 stage plays and 957 short stories.

Wallace became chairman of the Press Club which to this day holds an annual Edgar Wallace Award, rewarding 'excellence in writing'.

Diagnosed with diabetes his health deteriorated and he soon entered a coma and died of his condition and double pneumonia on the 7th of February 1932 in North Maple Drive, Beverly Hills. He was buried near his home in England at Chalklands, Bourne End, in Buckinghamshire.

Index of Contents

CHAPTER I

THE WOMAN OF THE LORELEI

The director of field information whose office is in Kaiser-Wilhelm-Strasse pressed a bell on his table and a smart young officer appeared at the door and saluted.

"Come in, Von Brun," said the director, scratching his white head. "Where and what is San Romino?"

"It is a republic within the Italian frontier, Herr Direktor."

"Is it at war with us?"

The officer smiled.

"I believe so."

"Has it an army?"

"A platoon—perhaps a company."

The director examined the documents in his hand.

"Read these," he said, and handed the papers to his subordinate. "They have just come from the foreign office."

The first letter was an official covering note begging his excellency to file the inclosed document, and informing him that all future reference to this or any correspondence relating to this should bear the indicator K. K. O. G. (1) 74479.

Lieut. von Brun turned this and read the paper beneath.

It bore the royal arms of Andalusia and informed the imperial German government that the Spanish ambassador had been requested by the government concerned to notify the imperial general staff that:

"An aviation squadron has been formed for special duties. The airplanes of this squadron will bear in addition to the rings of red, white and blue, an emblem representing the ace of clubs within a five-pointed star. Though it is not anticipated that any members of this squadron will be taken prisoners, it is notified that for the purpose of administration this corps will be attached to the army of the republic of San Romino."

The young officer handed the papers back to his chief with a nod.

"Units of this squadron have already been seen, Herr Direktor," he said. "One of their machines descended outside Frankfurt last week, and the aviator fought to the death."

"Fought to the death—how?"

The officer shrugged his shoulders. "He refused to surrender, burned his machine and defended himself with his revolver—and shot himself with his last cartridge."

"So? What was he doing over Frankfurt—ah. I remember! He was the man that bombed the house of Prince Zutterfurst."

The officer nodded.

"So!" said the director again, "that is queer; I thought at the time—a private vendetta, yes? But it was absurd—so I thought, but now! It is not expected that any members of the squadron will be taken prisoners. So!"

That night every German corps on the western front received a precautionary warning to look out for the squadron of the Ace who was officially designated "dangerous."

The umpty-eighth raiding squadron of the Independent Force. R. A. F.—commonly called the "strafes"—returning from a daylight stunt over Mannheim, met two fast Caproni-Moranes, painted dead black, as are night-bombing machines, and decorated with strange devices.

Craig, leader of the strafe squadron, signaled "Good hunting," and roared through the speaking tube which connected him with his gunner:

"Fee-fo-fi-fum! What's their stunt?"

"They've got a friend on the Rhine," wheezed the gunner—the Mannheim defenses had used gas shells and he did not feel conversational.

Archie gunners watched the high-flying fleet pass and speculated upon their errand.

"Nobody's darlings," explained a veteran to a newly joined subaltern, "you have to be careful with those fellows. They never notify you when they are coming over—but they have no grouch against you if you shell 'em. The ninety-fourth brought one down the other day, luckily without killing the pilot. He congratulated the gunner on his good practice! An American fellow named Trenchard—twenty-seven, and as a gray as a badger!"

"But what are they—British or American?"

"Everything. They have an airdrome behind the French line somewhere. It's a sort of foreign legion as far as I can gather."

The two planes kept company to a point on the Moselle southwest of Coblenz where the first Rhine barrage is sited. Before this they turned northward. Two chaser machines of a patrol fell to attack the right wing of the formation and the right flanker turned to meet the charge. His gun was in reality three guns under one control, and the savage burst of fire which greeted the nearest of the attackers sprayed nacelle, wing and fuselage. It was as though a spadeful of nickel had been thrown in the face of the assailant, but thrown with such a velocity that every pellet ripped and tore through canvas, steel and bone—

The attacker dropped sideways and the flanker zoomed up to meet his second enemy, but that gentleman was dropping straight for earth and the cover of the barrage.

"Cowardly custard!" mocked the flanker and came back to his position.

The flight bore to the left of Coblenz avoiding the wild and furious barrage which ranged the town, crossed the Rhine south of Neuwied, turned and followed the Nassau bank again, keeping clear of Coblenz and treating with proper contempt the feeble barrage of Ems.

There was no possibility of mistaking Oberwesel. The Rhine was low and the brown scars of the "Seven Virgins" showed clear in the silvery thread.

A signal from the leader and the machines began their glide down. The good citizens of Oberwesel—scurrying specks of humanity, like slow ants they looked from 5,000 feet—need not dive to their cellars and their dugouts. Smith, the leader, adjusting his camera could see a confused procession of these ants streaming to the Frauenkirche, but his objective was north of the town. His camera was pointed to a building which evidently stood on a spur of hill. It stood out clearly against the dark background, with its wings and annexes and courtyards for all the world like the wards of a white key.

He strained his eyes down and on the very edge of the building, the edge which by its regularity of outline was apparently the façade. He thought he detected a flutter of something white and pressed the trigger of his camera.

The flight was rising again as it passed over Oberwesel, but the quaking citizens did not know this and were still sitting tight in their cellars when the two machines were following the Moselle on their homeward run.

The mess of the Ace High was a rambling old farmhouse, the thick walls of which had been laid together in the days of Louis Quatorze. The interior had been transformed by a firm of Paris decorators—to the scandal of the army—so that it resembled nothing so much as a modern clubhouse built and decorated to convey the illusion that it was a farmhouse interior.

Before the house was a big lawn and great flower beds that blazed gorgeously. Beyond the trim hedge were the flats and camouflaged hangars.

On an evening when the sky was orange and crimson and laced with purple clouds, four men sat about a table placed on the lawn and drank syrups from long ice-packed glasses.

They wore the dark-gray uniforms of the squadron, and none wore any badge of rank which was visible to the observer.

Outsiders never joked with "Nobody's Darlings." It was said that they had no sense of humor, but those who said as much did not know them. They did not smile easily, it is true. For example it took a great deal to bring a smile to the eyes of New Trenchard, some time treasurer to the Ohio Trading Corporation. He had stopped smiling when he pulled his wife and baby daughter from beneath the overturned lifeboat of the "Lusitania" and found them both dead. He landed in Liverpool two nights later, cabled his president his resignation, and joined the Fifty-seventh Middlesex regiment, or, as the army calls them. "The Die-Hards."

Pink-faced little Gregory with his absurd mustache had had a sense of humor once, but it had stopped working when he found the girl he loved lying on a mortuary slab between a dead policeman and a woman of the streets—it was somewhat difficult to distinguish one from the other because the Zeppelin bomb which killed them fell less than a dozen yards away.

Victor Beauclerc was ordinarily a cheerful, volatile soul, and there were times when he forgot the look in the eyes of his father and two young brothers when the Germans led them out of the stable yard of the Hôtel de Brabant at Visé to execution. Other members of the squadron had other reasons for this taciturnity, and all those reasons went back to the hairy men who followed Attila across the steppes of central Europe.

"We're now officially recognized." said the man with the twinkling eyes, "but it took a lot of working. The British think we're irregular. The Americans secretly approve, but are in holy terror that we shall be regarded as American eccentrics. The French, bless their romantic hearts, are enthusiastic, but must have the approval of their allies. The Belgians are too dispirited to worry. The Italians too busy to care. As for the president of San Romino, he was tickled to death."

"Where is San Romino, anyway, Dexter?" asked Trenchard. "Is there such a place, or is it a sort of Ruritania?"

Dexter laughed softly.

"San Romino is the smallest republic on earth. It has an army of twenty and a police force of twenty, which means that in time of peace the army are cops and in time of war the cops are soldiers. But it is a sure-enough republic, has a star-spangled minister at the court of St. James, has treaties with foreign powers, and solemnly declared war when Italy came in—would have declared war before according to the president, but for the fear of embarrassing the Italian government."

Little Gregory giggled and gulped at his syrup.

"It's a wonderful little country, perched high in the mountains, almost inaccessible and about as big as New York was in the eighties. The president was delighted. He has opened a record office for the squadron and voted us one hundred thousand lira."

"What is this business costing you, Dexter?" asked Trenchard abruptly.

The man with the laughing eyes pulled steadily at his cigar before he answered.

"When my lamented father died." he said slowly, "he left me exactly ten million dollars. Since then I have added considerably to my fortune. For reasons which we will not discuss I am without heir"—he took his cigar from his teeth and flicked off the ash with great deliberation—"or hope," he went on. "I cannot tell you to a cent how much money I have, but It is all going into this. It will last a long time because three of our gracious allies—and by 'our' I mean San Romino—while officially expressing their doubt as to our scheme, have privately placed their aeroplane production at our disposal."

"Excellent man!" said Beauclerc. "For myself I shall need three machines before I attain to the summit of my ambition, which is to break a lance with a worthy gentleman named Von Koevisse, general of division, and a no less admirable and well-born Herr, the Hauptmann Maas of the One Hundred and Seventy-fifth Regiment."

He jumped to his feet and, shading eyes, looked up at the eastern sky.

"Smith's patrol," he said.

Two specks in the heavens grew in size and there came to the watchers the faint drone of their engines. Soon they were gliding at a violent angle earthward and presently two fur-coated pilots were moving slowly to the mess, exchanging views.

"Did you see all that wanted to see Smith?" asked Dexter.

The boy addressed nodded and beckoned a mess orderly.

"Tea for me—large drafts and mountainous piles of buttered toast, nothing more substantial or less," he said. "Yes I saw all I wanted to see. I'm not quite sure whether the flag was flying, I thought it was. I seemed to see a flutter of rag. Le Blou says he saw it too, but we'll know just as soon as we can develop the plates."

"You'll go—when?" asked Dexter.

"If the photograph shows the flag—tonight," said Smith quietly. "I'll take along a rack of bombs for Coblenz—afterwards."

"Quite," said Dexter. "Go along and develop those prints."

Half an hour later an orderly came to the lawn carrying a visiting card.

"Commander Trenther of the Royal Naval Air Service." read Dexter. "Hum. Show him out here."

The commander was a tall and cheerful young man, and in nowise depressed by the somewhat cool welcome he received.

"I know you people hate visitors," he smiled. "In fact, your glorious unsociability is greatly admired by the army. But I've come down especially from Dunkirk to see you about a recruit."

Dexter's grave eyes were fixed on the visitor, and he did not speak.

"The fact is, colonel"—he paused suggestively—"I'm fearfully ignorant, but I don't know your rank."

"Anything you like—corporal—first mate—field marshal—but go ahead," said Dexter.

"The fact is, one of our fellows has been hit rather hard. He was a clerk in an English office in Berlin and when war broke out he was on leave in England, his young wife being In Germany. I can't tell you the whole ghastly story, but apparently the Boche got to know that her husband was one of the raiding party which bombed Karlsruhe other day. It happened that the unfortunate woman was in Karlsruhe when the raid took place. That was enough, they tried her by court-martial, charging her with having made signals to the raiders—and shot her."

Dexter nodded.

"I would not have come to you if he had taken it raving, but he's not the crazy kind. He wants bigger work than we can give him—more individual work—will you take him?"

It was at this moment that Smith came of the mess.

"I say," he called, "that flag was all right. The photograph shows—"

He stopped dead.

Commander Trenther was on his feet staring at him.

"Why Bennett!" gasped the naval officer.

The man called Smith stood as though turned to stone.

"I'm afraid you've made a mistake," he said, "my name is Smith."

"Nonsense! You're Lieutenant Commander Bennett—my dear chap, you don't suppose I believed the charge, do you?"

"My name is Smith." smiled the other; "will you excuse me?"

He turned quickly and walked back into the mess.

"That's Bennett." said the officer vigorously. "I'd swear to him—poor chap! He was court-martialed in the early days of the war—gave some woman or other particulars of the new fire control. He pleaded guilty, but got off on some technical error in the indictment."

Dexter's smile was one of polite amusement.

"My dear commander, I have known Smith all my life—even longer. I knew him in a former incarnation when he was the only Smith in the world. Feel yourself all over, dear lad, you're not quite—er—"

The officer looked at him incredulously.

"But," he insisted. I served with Bennett on the same ship—it's the same man."

"My dear fellow!" murmured Dexter in protest. "Forget all about It—what is the name of this good sportsman you are sending to us, and"—he looked the other in the eye—"and what name will he call himself by?"

The commander opened his mouth to speak, but closed it again without saying what he intended.

"I see." he said quietly. "I'm afraid I'm rather a fool. Forgive me."

Dexter dropped his big hand on the officer's shoulder.

"Smith or Bennett," he said solemnly, "pray for him this night!"

The Baroness von Stromberg und Hasenbach lay on the big sofa in the salon of Schloss Lorelei, reading by the shaded light of a silver standard lamp conveniently placed behind her head.

A little Oriental table thickly inlaid with silver stood at hand and held the coffee set.

One dainty slipper had fallen off exposing the foot which inspired the poet Grimwald to his most daring composition and had inspired less poetical subalterns of the guards to wordless ecstasy.

The baron, a stout man wearing the uniform which marked him as a member of the great general staff, sat in a deep armchair, his back to her, less an act of discourtesy than a desire to read the Lokalanzeiger by the one light in the salon.

He put the paper down and stood up listening. Then he walked to the long windows and pulled the curtains a little closer.

"Bombs," he said. "Coblenz, of course. It's a good moon for night flying. Why on earth we started this damnable town raiding I don't know. Curse the war; it has lasted too long," he grumbled, "the only people who make money out of it are the Jews of Frankfurt and profiteers. Do you realise that there isn't ten thousand marks in the bank? My love," he shook his head, "I wish—"

"That I was bringing more money into your account?" she smiled. "Really, you are unreasonable."

"I know, I know," he said hastily. "These infernal raids are getting on my nerves."

"They won't come here," said the girl on the sofa lazily. "We had two over this afternoon, but they did nothing. Hermann says the Bürger of Oberwesel were beside themselves with fright."

"A reconnaissance," grumbled the baron, brushing up his yellow mustache with a quick jerk of his hand. "There go the guns again—do you hear them?"

"For heaven's sake, sit down!"

He looked down at her with a smile.

"Gen. von Steinbach was saying today that he had never seen you looking so beautiful, except when you came back from England to marry your devoted slave, as you were when he saw you last week," he said.

The girl showed her white teeth in a grimace of distaste.

"He thought I was beautiful because I brought him rich treasures of information—hark!"

She raised her hand.

"Guns!"

She shook her bead.

"No—It is the Rhine passing the Lorelei—it sounds very near tonight—do you ever realize how appropriately placed this house is?"

"Appropriate—how?"

She laughed up at him.

"I am thinking of my work in England—the work that made Gen. von. Steinbach think I was so beautiful. And I was connecting it with the legend of the Lorelei."

He looked at her blankly.

"I don't see the connection, my gracious lady. As I remember the legend, which I do through Heine's poem, it is the story of a fairy who lived on the Lorelei and lured seamen to their ruin at the foot of the precipice."

She picked up her book again with an impatient little twist of her shoulder.

"You are stupid, Adolph," she said, and with a shrug of his shoulders he settled down into his chair and took up his paper.

"Why do you fidget?" she asked presently.

"There's an aeroplane somewhere about," he said. "Do you mind switching out the light? I want to go on to the balcony and listen."

She stretched up and turned out the light and be stumbled forward and pulled back the curtains. The French windows were open and he stepped out on to the stone balcony.

He heard the drone of engines coming nearer and nearer, but though he searched the moonlit heavens there was no sign of a machine. Then the droning ceased altogether and he came back to the room with an apology.

"Are you satisfied?" she asked snapping the light on again. "Or will you presently hear other noises?"

"My love, I am a soldier, therefore, I am nervous," he said.

It was she who broke the silence which followed.

"Do you think less of me, darling, for taking money?" she asked suddenly.

"For what—are you still thinking of your unfortunate mariners—thunder and lightning! I begin to feel jealous of those fellows! No, my love! You did the work of a good German and you deserved good German payment. Have I reason to complain—O savior of the house of Stromberg? Did I not myself serve five years in the American and English branches of our intelligence department? What happened to the men, by the way?"

"They were shot, I think," she said carelessly.

"Only one."

"How did you know?" she asked in surprise.

"I didn't speak," said her husband.

She twisted round on the sofa so as to look over its head.

"I said they were shot and you said—"

"Only one," said the same voice.

She sat up peering through the gloom past her husband. A man in a close-fitting leather suit stood in the opening of the window curtains. There was a Browning in each of his hands.

The baron had followed the direction of his wife's eyes and now saw the intruder.

"Who are you?" he croaked.

The man in the window smiled crookedly.

"I am the one who wasn't shot." he said.

The girl sat, her lips apart, her eyes staring, her face the color of ashes.

"Good evening, Evelyn," The man called Smith bowed in her direction. "I call you by the name I knew you and loved you by. The name I whispered to you when I held you in my arms and your little hands were clasped about my neck. It is the name, I think, I called you that night when like a drunkard intoxicated with fool love, I told you all there was to be told about the Collins Fire Control."

She did not answer. Her husband babbled into a froth of incoherent sound, but the man called Smith silenced him with a gesture.

"What my friend Lieutenant Bolivar called you, I cannot say," Smith went on evenly. "I did not know that you and he were also lovers, and that he paid the price with artless tittle-tattle concerning our mobilization plans. They shot him, Evelyn, on the quarterdeck of the flagship.

"I've been waiting for you for three years," he went on. "I know you—both. It all came out at my court-martial. You were notorious spies in spite of your high position, in spite of your grand state and the flag that flies over your castle when you are in residence. It wasn't only me—it wasn't only poor Bolivar; you spent two years in England calling yourself Evelyn Stromberg and posing as a concert singer, worming your way into the confidence of foolish men and gullible boys. The money you brought to your damned husband was blood money—the price of treachery to those who loved you. You bought his moth-eaten barony with the tears of mothers and the shame of fathers—and when the war is over you will go back again to—"

"No, no! No, no!" She was on her knees babbling wildly. "No, Eric—you will forgive—"

He shot her from where he stood and she died instantly.

Then he walked back to his machine through the night and burned it.

They found him dead by its side, a pistol in his hand. And the woven badge of the Ace High upon his breast was sent to field information (B) for identification and report.

CHAPTER II

LOVING HEART AND THE MAN WITH THE CHARMED LIFE

Dexter, commandant of the Ace High, had a picture gallery in his big, oak-paneled office. The pictures were of young men in the uniform of the squadron. These photographs were framed in polished ebony, and were hung in a line with the eye of the chief.

On a smaller silver tablet laid into the frame was engraved the pilot's name and the day he died. For when a member of the squadron failed to return from patrol he was accounted dead. The companions of the Ace High were not taken prisoners.

Sethley, forced by defective engines to land at Saarbrücken, fought off two companies of the Two Hundred and Seventy-first regiment with his machine guns until he was killed. Boulanger, shot down from the air and desperately wounded, kept his captors at bay with a magazine pistol and used the last shot for himself.

When little Ed Cornell went out in the fulfillment of his vendetta to kill Colonel Baron von Eissen, who had commanded the brigade which had occupied Badonvillers—Cornell's wife was a French girl and was visiting her relations in eastern France when the war broke out—he, too was shot down from the air. He had left von Eissen's headquarters a smoking ruin, so his heart was at peace, and when he stepped from his damaged machine and faced the charging squadron of Uhlans he had no regrets. Four horsemen went down before the long lances got him through the heart.

That was the way of the Ace High—the law written or unwritten.

Dexter, a cigar between his teeth, rendering his daily report to the chief of the tiny republic in whose nominal service he was, never referred to his men as missing. If six days elapsed and they did not return, he reported, employing the terminology of his Latin chief that such and such a one had "fallen for the liberty of the world."

So he reported Brandon Jackson when he fell in flames by Havrincourt Forest, which the English airman has christened "Mossy-face Wood." He might have added in his private record book that the slayer was "Loving Heart," but he had not heard that German's nickname until Hooky came to the squadron.

Dexter said, some time before that final fight in which he met his mortal enemy, that the history of the Companions of the Ace High began with the coming of Pilot Hooky Patterson.

It is true that poets and pilots are born and not made; it is true that one man's meat is another man's poison, and that you cannot put a square peg in a round hole—indeed, the appalling truthfulness of moth-eaten tags is one the most saddening discoveries of life.

Hooky was a born pilot; that he was poison to the said commanders of the Seven Hundred and Seventy-fourth British Squadron, to the unusually amiable Captain Bouvergenge of the Nine hundred and Thirty-first French Escadrille, and to the irascible chief of United States bombing squadron 631 was an indubitable fact.

Beckworth came over from the United States headquarters flying what the British call a "Liberty Bond," and landed before the mess of the Ace High.

"See here, Dexter, I've got a boy for you," he said, advancing with outstretched hands to the gray commandant.

"Well, you seem in a mighty hurry to get rid of him."

Captain Beckworth groaned.

"Hurry is hardly the word; he's a good boy, Dexter, make no mistake about that—full of pep and the dandiest pilot you ever saw. Belongs to one of the New England families and has all the money in the world. If he ever met fear he'd pass it without knowing what it looked, like, and he hasn't an enemy in the world."

"H'm," said Dexter, "that's hardly a qualification, is it? You know why I formed this squadron. Beckworth, these boys of mine are the original suicide club. We are men with scores to settle—general and individual."

"I thought you worked with the French?"

Dexter nodded.

"We work with the British, too, when they want us—we formed the left-wing guard of the big raid they had on Coblenz this morning. But generally, we're working out our own salvation and helping along Intelligence. There's no room—I tell you frankly—there's no room in the squadron for a boy without some purpose even if he's the dandiest pilot that ever crashed a 'pup.'"

Beckworth's face fell.

"Well, you were my last hope. The British wouldn't keep him—God knows I don't blame them. The French turned him over to us and wept with relief. There's nothing wrong with the boy—a certain extravagance of language—but you can't tell how much of that is sheer jollying and this habit of wandering."

"Wandering?" asked the puzzled Dexter.

"That's it; we call him Hooky because he just goes off on his own. I've seen him leave formation to chase a hawk over the Black Forest. He's been up in the middle of the night to see the sun dawn on the Vosges—he's taken joy rides into the Alps for the sensation of landing on the top of Mount Blanc. It took ten guides a week to get the machine down, and then they had to dig it out of the snow. But that boys' a fighter, Dexter. He can shoot the dope off a tail-plane, as the saying goes. If he gets his sights on a Hun that Hun is a casualty. It's the humdrum of the work that breaks him."

Dexter thrust his hands into the capacious pockets of his jacket.

"Does he want to come?"

"He's crazy to come. I had to beg him not to follow me—who's that?"

Dexter stood up, shading his eyes.

Through the clear blue of the sky an airplane was descending. But it was a kind of descent which is not encouraged. It looped and looped like a big hoop descending invisible stairs. At five thousand feet the looping ceased and the windmills began. Wing over wing in simulated helplessness the little plane fell until it came round on a vertical bank, the silent engines roared forth again, and with his nose down the pilot fell into a spinning nose dive.

"That's Hooky," said Beckworth dismally.

The machine pancaked over the mess, turned sharply, and glided to the side of Beckworth's plane.

"That's Hooky," said Beckworth again.

The young man who leaped to the ground was bareheaded. He stopped to line the machine so that its landing wheels cleared a little patch of long grass.

"Weight six hundred and sixty pounds: but he could lift a house," said the gloomy Beckworth.

Hooky Patterson came up with long strides. There was nothing abnormal in his appearance. He was a good-looking boy, with a clear, tanned skin and gray, deep-set eyes. His height was something in the region of six feet, the breadth of his shoulders spoke of extraordinary strength.

"Shake hands with Major Dexter, Hooky," said Beckworth soberly. "He's between you and a court-martial."

Dexter's hand was gripped as in a vise, and a pair of eager, laughing eyes searched his.

"You're taking me. Major?"

"Well—"

"Ah, come on! Major. You've gotter have me! Major, I'll buy the squadron ten beautiful buses with Louise Quinze fittin's—ah, colonel, behave! Colonel, I've got a sure 'nough enemy—I lay for him every time I remember. He lives over behind Mossy-face Wood an' I call him 'Loving Heart' because of his wonderful smile. I'm giving it to you straight, Colonel."

He thrust his arm through Dexter's and turned to his dumbfounded chief.

"Get the boys to send my baggage over, dear old—sir. Tell 'em if they see me rovin' round that I'm on special service an' thank you for all you've done."

He grasped the officers' reluctant hand.

"Now, listen."

Dexter gently disengaged himself.

"I'm taking you, Patterson."

"Call me Hooky," pleaded the young man; "let's start fair and friendly. Call me Hooky."

Dexter's eyes gleamed his secret merriment.

"I'm taking you because I think you may be useful, and because if I don't take you I can see your finish. You have no more idea of discipline—"

"Ah, don't say it!" murmured Hooky.

"—than a wild cat. You will contribute ten thousand dollars to the common fund of the squadron, you will replace all machines that you crash, and you will be forgiven everything—except the desertion of your comrades in the hour of their need."

Hooky Patterson, watching him, sensed the reality of the companionship.

"We have a peculiar function," Dexter went on; "you are not bound by any promise or oath save to the republic in whose service we are. If you fail us I shall ask you to go, for you will have broken faith with the living who will die and the dead who everlastingly live in our hearts."

"I understand, sir," said Hooky in a low voice.

"Now fly back your machine and report to me tomorrow."

Obediently, even meekly, the young man strode to his little scout and hoisted himself to the pilot's seat. The mechanics who had, as a matter of routine, grouped themselves about the two airplanes, spun the propeller, and in a few seconds the scout was zooming up to the blue.

The two men watched, then—

"He's not going home, darn him! He's on a joy ride," snapped Beckworth.

The tiny machine had turned eastward and was soon a disappearing speck in the skies.

"Who is Loving Heart with the smile—one of Hooky's brilliant flights of imagination?"

Captain Beckworth was drawing on his gauntlet and strapping his sleeves preparatory to taking his departure. He made a little grimace.

"I wish he were," he said. "He got one of my best boys yesterday—shot him when he was crippled, though he managed to make the aerodrome. Löwenhardt is the man; you've heard of him?"

"Löwenhardt!" Dexter, watching the vanishing Hooky, jerked round. "What has he got against Löwenhardt?"

Beckworth eyed the other in surprise.

"Friend of yours?"

Dexter nodded grimly.

"We're all little friends of Loving Heart," he said. "I don't know what pull that fellow's got, but he shoots from cover every time. He's a cripple-chaser, a ground-strafer—there's not a soft, safe job in the imperial air service that that boy doesn't go after. You've never seen him in a circus, have you?"

Beckworth shook his head.

"The English say that he never does a patrol; they think that 'Löwenhardt' is a name which disguises a German princeling. Have you got anything on him?"

Dexter puffed at his cigar.

"Jackson of my squadron developed engine trouble on the other side of Mossy-face Wood and had to make a forced landing. Somebody followed him down and shot him sitting, that's all. I have reason to believe that somebody was Löwenhardt. Machine-gunned him when the boy had landed. Our boys don't expect to be taken alive, but we like then to have a chance."

"The swine!"

Dexter laughed shortly.

"He's that, all right. I sent a flight over the same night, and we dropped De Courland in a parachute with orders to settle accounts with Loving Heart, but he'd gone on leave. De Courland got back through our lines with a whole lot of information about him. He dodged from squadron to squadron. He's no prince, believe me! He's a low down Brunswicker in the Intelligence Bureau of the Great General Staff. He directs the landings of spies on our side of the line and is a pretty important fellow, and even generals and people are scared of him—you see, he works directly in conjunction with the chiefs of the German army and that gives him a pull. What has Hooky got against him?"

"Ask him," smiled Beckwith. "Hooky neither goes where he's sent nor reports what he sees. That boy's full of good information, and he's just scared to death that you'll find it out and make him write it!"

In the morning came Hooky Patterson, surprisingly punctual, driving a six-cylinder car—his own property, which, in some mysterious fashion, he had succeeded in getting into France—which was stacked with baggage.

"Here's my check and here I am, commander of the faithful," said Hooky breathlessly, "a Bristol or a Curtiss scout is my passion and hobby; Spads I adore, the British B-6 I abominate. Give me," he said, drawing up a chair and seating himself without invitation, "give me something with a stagger, something with short wings and a quick rise, something that loops if you breathe on the control, and I will darken the skies with falling Huns!"

Dexter looked curiously into the eager face, and youth and the fanatical faith of youth shone in the gray eyes. There was laughter, too—a spring of sheer animal joy that bubbled and frothed to the surface. He was one of those rare creatures whose laughter turns in upon themselves and passes through a fiery test which burns out all malice and uncharity.

There were no eyes like these in the squadron. There were eyes quiet, suspicious; eyes somber and smoldering: eyes tired with the pain of thought and made sorrowful by unsleeping memories—

"Boy," he said gently, "it somehow comes upon me that you don't belong here."

"Don't belong—"

Dexter shook his gray head.

"I don't want to depress you, but the men who join this squadron are doomed—there's no escape—"

"See here, colonel!" The boy was on his feet, and his big hand dropped familiarly on his superior's shoulder—for Hooky Patterson placed military discipline among the amusing jokes of life. "You can't scare me; no, sir! I'm coming through this war alive and happy. I'm too good to die, colonel. I just feel right here in the pericardium a most wonderful hunch that I've got a charmed life. Colonel, the fairies smiled on my birth—they just laughed 'emselves ill! Why, sir, sometimes way up there," he jerked his head to the roof, but was apparently indicating the high heavens, "when I'm feeling lonesome and fine watchin' the stars go out and the sun peekin' up and the first light of day resting on the clouds like a fiery dew—I've, got that live feeling so intense that I pity the moon that's dead and the earth that'll go out in a few paltry billions of years!"

Dexter's eyes did not leave the boy's face. Then he rose.

"Come here," he said.

He walked to the wall where his picture gallery hung and pointed to the portrait of a man—a man with a strong face and a breadth of shoulder rivaling Hooky's.

"Who is he?" he asked. "I seem to know him."

He read the inscription on the silver plate beneath:

"OLIVER G. WEATHERBY.
Died March 17, 1917."

"Weatherby?" Hooky shook his head. "I don't remember him—and yet—"

Dexter lit a new cigar.

"That is the man with the charmed life," he said with a little smile. "He came to me in January before America was in the war. Most of this squadron have a grievance and most of them tell me all about it. Weatherby never spoke of his. He came from somewhere in the state of Illinois and brought letters of introduction from home. I should have turned him over to the French, but he was a pretty good pilot and gave me to understand he wanted our kind of work. Well, we tried him out, sent him on a patrol, and he came back full of news. Then we tried him on escort work and he made good. You say you've a charmed life! I tell you that man took every risk there was and came through it all untouched. He'd go through a ring of shrapnel and sort of trample down the fire. It was uncanny. Richthofen and his circus got him circled once, and the airman wasn't born that could break through that cordon, but it melted for Weatherby. He landed in Germany in daylight—a French patrol saw him go down within a mile of Coblenz—and got away again.

"And then one day he went over the German lines and never came back again. He was last seen to the south of Metz. His machine was shot down a week later by the French. It had been captured intact by the Germans and flown by them over our lines. We had a message dropped by a German airplane saying: Lieut. Weatherby is dead. And that is all."

Hooky Patterson was silent.

"Well, I guess he hadn't my hunch," he said at last, and Dexter laughed.

"You're invincible, Hooky," he said. "Here is your badge—you will share quarters with Beauclerc, and you'll go left cover to all escorting squadrons—if we can find you when you're wanted."

Hooky was darting from the room— his every movement was in double time—when Dexter called him.

'By the way, Patterson, what have you got on Löwenhardt?"

"Loving Heart?"

The boy frowned in an effort of memory, for he had forgotten his feud.

"Oh, Loving Heart! Sure—he's a low-down fighter, that fellow; he shot me up with explosive bullets, darn him. I'll go right along and get him!"

But nearly a month passed before Loving Heart came back to the Cambrai sector.

Whatever might be said against him this is sure:

Loving Heart with the smile had no false ideas as to his own merits. He knew, for example, that to tackle a patrol of the Umpty-ninth squadron, United States Flying corps, single-handed, would be magnificent, but not, as he understood it, war. To take on four American aces making their way back to their aerodrome after a big strafe was not war, either, and it is remarkable that he should have committed so fatal an error. It is true that three of the four were coasting through a cloud at eighteen thousand feet, looking for an Albatross which had coyly retired from observation and that the fourth was lame and losing height. The pilot's right leg, moreover, was hanging helpless among the controls, and the pilot, with ashen face, was reserving his last ounce of strength and energy to land behind the British lines. Him Loving Heart saw and dropped swiftly to the attack. The stricken pilot looked up with a little grin, the sort of smile with which brave men face the certainty of death, and let fly a burst at fifty yards, working his machine gun with the one hand which was not wholly shot to pieces.

Loving Heart came into a vertical bank—no unskilled maneuver from a nose dive—and spun around to get upon the cripple's tail.

He was most comfortably placed and was mentally notching his death tally when a cold shiver passed along his spine and he looked up.

The three uncrippled scouts were dropping to him. He had a glimpse of three capital H's turned on their sides.

Something ripped through the canvas of the left lower plane.

Loving Heart pushed his lever forward and fell steeply, firing red signal balls to the anti-aircraft batteries below.

He flattened out and landed before he looked up. Four little scouts were moving westward, and one of them was indulging in aerobatics which were undoubtedly intended to be insulting. That night Loving Heart's squadron commander made his report to grand headquarters, and grand headquarters duly announced:

Capt. von Löwenhardt engaged four hostile scouts single-handed, shooting one down in flames and forcing the other three to retreat precipitately. This is Capt. von Löwenhardt's seventeenth aerial victory.

The next morning Herr Hauptmann von Löwenhardt rose before dawn, for he had work of considerable importance to carry out. At a height of sixteen thousand feet he flew westward toward a little village, where one of his intelligence officers had his headquarters.

The officer in question was known to the French as an innocent storekeeper with a robust faith in the victory of the Allies. To Löwenhardt he was known as Franz Durmanberg. The airman read the signal— he had to fly directly over the high-walled yard to read the message which two triangles of colored lights spelled—and turned southward as the day was breaking, to collect such gossip as might be conveyed by a charcoal burner on the edge of Cotteret Forest.

Here the medium of information was more ingenious. Saplings cut and laid at certain angles spelled "4714—1239," which might be translated into: "47th Division gone to 14 sector. 12th Division gone to 39 sector."

Again Löwenhardt swung round and followed the course of the Aisne to north of Rheims. He looked at his watch—he was exactly on time; at his altitude indicator—he was at the right height. Then he caught the flash twenty miles westward. It was the flash of the sun striking a fanlight at an angle. Six times it flashed as though some awkward concierge were tugging at the cords which worked the hinged window, and Löwenhardt read the message and jotted it on the pad which was strapped to his knee.

Then he turned for home, for to the left and right were enemy machines and the French guns by Craonne were shelling him. He crossed the dark stretch of the Gobain Forest, following the railway east of St. Quentin.

He was over Ribemont when the attack came. It came most unexpectedly from the east. Out of the blue dropped a solitary scout. Its markings were invisible, but its obvious intentions were beyond doubt.

Löwenhardt fingered his signal pistol and looked over the side. He was flying at well over ten thousand feet, which is a dangerous height if you wish to avoid battle. He pushed his nose down and dropped into a steep dive, glancing upward over his shoulder at his opponent,

His attacker changed his course slightly and in so doing one wing tipped up and exposed its markings. Löwenhardt's eyes narrowed behind the mica goggles and he felt a little grip at his heart, for within the familiar circle was the sign of the Ace and the star.

He pushed the muzzle of his signal pistol over the side of the fuselage and pulled the trigger, but the weapon missed fire.

A hail of bullets whizzed past him: something hit his leather helmet and ripped it off, carrying away his goggles.

Hooky—blessed Providence and rewarded for early rising—saw the effect of the shot and thought he had killed his man, for immediately the nose of the German machine went down and this time it fell steeply, but it was under control. Löwenhardt must have been rattled by the shot, for presently he pulled his big scout out of the dive before she was within gliding distance and his pursuer swept past him.

He fired a burst as the scout heeled over and saw an outer strut fly. He fired again and banked to maneuver out of range. It was precisely that moment that his enemy chose to zoom up to meet him, and for a second the two machines, racing at one hundred miles an hour, were in a parallel course.

Hooky's gun covered his man—he waited the infinitesimal fraction of a second for Löwenhardt to lift his head. Then it showered, and for yet another infinitesimal space the American hesitated. In the clear light of the morning they glared at one another.

Löwenhardt pushed the control to the left, but before the wing could rise and hide him the Lewis gun roared and Loving Heart was dead.

"I 'knew' I'd seen that face before," said Hooky, staring down at the tumbling machine, and in his mind's eyes was the photograph of "Oliver G. Weatherby," whose immunity from German airmen and German guns had been the wonder of the western front.

Dexter listened in silence to the picturesque narrative—for Hooky had the descriptive gift and he detailed not only the fight but its every environment and background—and when he had finished, the commandant said simply:

"There's a vacant frame in the office, Hooky—see that you keep out of it!"

CHAPTER III

THE KURT OF HONOR

They called Kurt of Wennigen the Kurt of Honor, and Sullivan, who was chargé d'affaires at the embassy for a long time, has left it on record that he was the only gentleman in Germany.

That may or may not be true, but Dexter, of the Ace High Squadron, who had fought the prince until his only gun jammed, always said: "There are Germans and Germans—but I only met the Germans till I met Kurt of Wennigen."

For Kurt, seeing his enemy's helplessness and recognizing that he was the victim of bad luck, had broken off the fight with a cheery wave of his hand and had glided around in search of somebody better able to defend himself.

They called him the Kurt of Honor because he was the final arbiter in matters touching honorable dealing. In the days before the madness came, he was the Bayard of the German army, possessing a power surer than Von Hertzel's, more complete than that of his imperial highness.

He fought and killed Major Count von Rathskell on the nice question of an initial—the initial being that of a lady mentioned by Graf von Rathskell. He suffered close arrest in the fortress of Ingolstadt for killing Von Bernardi, the dispute arising out of a money-lending transaction in which Bernardi had acted as agent, and it is rumored that he had challenged a very high one, close indeed to the imperial successor, and that it had taken the united efforts of the imperial chancellor, backed by the minister of war and the chief of the general staff, to convince the army that the challenged highness could not in propriety accept such a challenge.

His mother, the old Duchess of Wennigen, held views which were not dissimilar to those of her austere son.

When Adolph of Karlsruhe came to spend the week-end with this lady, who was his aunt, the Seventeenth Corps Aerial Company of the Engineers let up four captive balloons, one at each corner of the house. These rose to the height of five hundred feet, and each was tethered by the fine steel cables in such a way that, in addition to the perpendicular wire, there were two at an angle. By this means there were formed four Saint Andrew Crosses of wire in the air. At night the cables were let out to a thousand feet.

The prince, smoking a cigarette, came out on the terrace to watch the lengthening and was satisfied.

"But, my dear Adolph," said the grand duchess with good-natured derision, "you do not imagine for one moment that these absurd people—what do you call them—the High Aces—"

"The Ace High Squadron," said the prince, making a little grimace as though the words hurt him, "yes, I mean all that I said. They will follow me and they will bomb me, or at least one of them will."

"You mean the American?"

The prince nodded.

The old woman looked at him keenly. "What have you done to him?"

The prince shrugged one shoulder impatiently. He was a sallow-faced young man with a trim dark mustache and the high cheek bones which are characteristic of the house of Karlsruhe.

"It's a long story," he said. "Anyway, Aunt Sophia, we know—a damned English prisoner who escaped from our cage at Sennelager saw it and found out my name—"

"Oh, that!"

The duchess understood. So many events had been crowded into the past two years that she had almost forgotten the story. It had to do with the war of East Prussia and an American girl who had been touring Germany and found herself in Gumbingen when the Russian tide of invasion had swept through the pleasure ground of the junkers. The Russians had treated the girl with consideration and courtesy, and then Hindenburg's army had appeared and had swept Samsonov into the Masurian Lakes. From thence onward all trace of Jean Lexington had been lost.

Then one evening a British prisoner who had escaped from Sennelager, while making his way by night to the Dutch frontier, had stopped at a big house to burgle food and clothing. He had seen a weeping girl and an insolent young officer in the uniform of the Prussian Guard, had caught a few words in a language he understood, such words as: "My good Miss Lexington—it is an honor that I, Adolph of Karlsruhe—" But had not realized that anything was very wrong.

At any rate, he could have done nothing, for he was unarmed and the darkness about the great house was filled with the voices of servants and orderlies. Nevertheless, on his arrival in England, he had spoken of this experience to the examiner who takes the statements of escaped prisoners, and the facts had been forwarded to the American embassy. More than this, they were published in the American press, and Prince Adolph had been summoned to great headquarters to give his version. He had certainly been in Gumbingen on the day the girl had vanished, it was as certainly possible that he, a great feudal lord commanding cavalry recruited from his own retainers, could compel their slavish obedience, and it was an undoubted fact that he was on his Westphalian estate on the very day the English soldier had seen him in conversation with the girl; but he denied all knowledge of her, produced his adjutant and his personal servants, who swore that they had no knowledge of her existence, and the matter was promptly dismissed as being the invention of a malicious prisoner of war.

This the grand duchess remembered, slowly swinging her fan.

"So the squadron believe that you—know." She was a shrewd old lady with a profound contempt for the Prussian branch of her family—she had been a Saxon princess before she came to Wennigen in the seventies. "And they're knights-errant—"

"It is one fellow," said the prince explosively, "one tradesman named Lane. Ah, yes, our intelligence have given me full particulars. A storekeeper! Without birth of any kind, it is monstrous!"

The grand duchess smiled coldly.

"Storekeepers have hearts, my dear Adolph, especially American storekeepers. Kurt, who knows America, says that many of them are college men and are quite well educated. This Lane was—"

Adolph of Wennigen controlled his temper as best he could. He could not consign Kurt to the devil for reasons.

"Affianced to Jean—Jean Lexington," he corrected himself hastily. "I call her Jean in my mind," he went on lamely, meeting the old woman's cold eyes. "She has become almost a real person to me—I have heard so much of the girl."

The grand duchess nodded and looked up at the four swaying balloons with their interlacing stays.

"And do you usually do—this sort of thing"—she jerked her head to the air trap —"wherever you are?"

He went red.

"Only when I am in bombing distance of the line," he said, licking his lips. "My father thinks it is wise, and the All-Highest-the-Same-Ones.* I am, as you know, the heir to the throne of Ahnt-Darmstadt and Karlsruhe."

[* Literal translation of the German term Allerhöchstdieselben. A reference to the Kaiser. A more understandable translation would be "His Supreme Highness Himself."]

She looked at him, noted the confusion and the shame, caught, for the first time, a momentary hint of his terror, and nodded.

A shrill bugle call split the evening air and the slim figure of the young prince went rigid.

"There is an enemy machine coming," he said thickly. "That is the signal. I have telephone connection with the Seventeenth Army Corps. May I take my leave, gracious lady?"

He did not wait for an answer, but pushed his way through the guests and into the great house. For he knew of cellars hewn in the solid rock which formed the foundations of Schloss Wennigen.

The duchess looked past her startled guests. With never a muscle moving, she turned back to the terrace and raised her lorgnette to survey the skies. The moon had risen at its full, but no moon gleams on the dead black of a night bomber. Those daring souls who had not melted away to the security of the house and who now stood in a semicircle about the grand old lady of Wennigen—here, without exception, were all the officers of the party—heard without seeing, the machine.

Snarl-zoo-o-o-snarl-zoo. Fitfully rising to a hateful buzz-saw howl, sinking to a complaining drone, the noise of the airplane drew nearer. Then a light appeared in the skies, a full blue bubble of light that grew in size and intensity until the whole countryside was illuminated with a brilliance that made the moonlight insignificant.

"Parachute flare, your serene highness," said a man's voice. "I suggest we stand close to the house."

But no bombs dropped. The noise of the airplane rose to a deafening and continuous thunder, and then they saw it circling like a gray moth shape in the light which the magnesium flare reflected back from the earth.

In such a light the four balloons were visible and the man in the big Spad could even see the metallic gleam of the wire guys.

He circled for half a minute and then began to climb westward. Presently the snarl was a drone and the drone a hum and then there was silence.

"Adolph's balloon guard was effective," said the grand duchess lightly, and beckoned her major-domo. "Keller, tell his serene highness that there is no further danger. You will probably find this serene highness in the Moselle vault."

On the Monday, the prince came to her boudoir to kiss hands on taking his leave.

"I fear I have given you a great deal of trouble," he said, but she cut him short.

"Adolph," her voice was like steel, "if this unfortunate American woman is in your keeping, marry her."

"Gracious lady!"

"Marry her, or I think this storekeeper will kill you sooner or later, but that is immaterial. What is to the point is this: that you should not bring the House of Princes into any worse odium than that in which they already are."

"I swear to you, dear aunt—"

"You lie," said the old woman quietly. "Get rid of that American girl by marriage or—"

"But she wouldn't marry me—she wouldn't—she wouldn't!" he burst forth.

"Oh!"

She got up, closed the folding doors which led from the outer reception room, and came back to her place by the gilt writing table where he had found her.

"Now tell me everything—where is she?"

The young man wiped his streaming brow with a shaky hand.

"You swear you won't tell—my God! If the All-Highest should know—"

"You overrate the humanity of the Hohenzollern," she scoffed. He shivered and seemed inclined to cross himself. "There was never a member of that house who would not regard your adventure as a joke. No, it is not William and his breed that I care for—it is for my own house. For the honor of my son, all of my race that has gone before, all that will come after. You'll tell me the truth or Kurt shall come to you and demand it."

His shaking hands went out in protest. Kurt of Wennigen, that slim gray colonel of cavalry, with his fanatical code and his wrist of steel....

"She's dead!" he blurted. "She died—in the lake at my castle in the Odenwald. I never harmed her, I swear it! I was afraid—after all the scandal, so I hid her in the Odenwald, and she escaped and Heinrich found her body in the Little Lake."

The old woman pursed her lips and looked past him.

"Go, now," she said.

"As God lives, gracious lady!"

"Go, now."

He left the castle plucking at his lips with nervous fingers. This was on a Monday. Adolph of Karlsruhe went back to his home and waited for a summons to great headquarters. As the days passed and no summons came his spirits rose. Ten days went by and Adolph came to army headquarters and was favorably received.

The companions of the Ace High were not a communicative body. Their conversation at such meals as they took together had mostly relation to the weather, the strength and the direction of the wind, for they were holding many secrets besides those private grievances which grew in every heart save one.

The most eccentric of organizations have a tendency to form part of an ordered system contributing in their very eccentricity to the rounded completeness of the general plan. The orbit of the companions of the Ace High, nominally owing allegiance to fifty square miles of an Italian republic, and actually a body privately organized by an American citizen, was gradually conforming to the movement of the greater body and was becoming if not absorbed by, at best moving with the big army machine.

More and more the aces were requisitioned for intelligence work. More and more frequently came the "A-a Confidential" to the Archie batteries telling them of strange machines which would fly over at extraordinary hours, and these warnings were in turn from French, British, and American headquarters.

Pilot Hooky Patterson, whose heart sang glad songs, and who emulated that Theocrite of whom Browning said:

Early morning, noon, and night
"Praise God!" said Theocrite.

supplied all the joyousness that the squadron knew.

"You sing in your sleep 'Ooky, truly!" complained little Beauclerc, his roommate. "Name of a pipe, you make chin wag eternally, truly!"

"Son of France," began Hooky.

"Belgium," corrected the other quickly.

"Pardon, you speak French—"

"You speak English, 'Ooky, yet you are not Scotch," said Beauclerc confusingly.

"Listen, brother," said Hooky Patterson, poising a large cup of steaming coffee, "you wonder why I sing. I will tell you—two nights ago I saw the moon rise over Cologne. Oh, the wonder of it!"

"Cologne!" It was Dexter, sitting at the head of the table. "I thought you were escorting the raid on Metz-Sablon?"

Hooky waved a lofty denial.

"Metz-Sablon bores me, colonel. No, sir, I joined an English squadron outside left. I didn't know where they were going, but I was good for four hundred miles, so I went along. My! I guess that English skipper was mad. He kept signaling to me, asking who I was. I just kept on answering 'O. K.' And it was fine! I flew low to get a better view—wonderful! You know how the cathedral towers rise, 'prayers frozen to stone' bathed in gray-green moonlight, and throwing mysterious shadows upon shadows deeper still. A symphony in green and purple—that's Cologne in the light of a full moon—and the English got two lovely bursts on the railway station!"

"I saw you."

It was Steve Lane, whose taciturnity was remarkable even in a community so sparing of speech as this, who spoke.

A grave young man with lined and haggard eyes, he now broke the silence of a week.

"I saw you coming over Trèves. You were a mile to the right of the squadron and losing height."

Hooky grinned and nodded and drank his coffee in one movement.

"Sure thing," he admitted. "I was parting company and trying to pick up the Metz-Sablon crowd, but I guess they must have gone on without me—and, anyway, I was down to my last pint of juice when I landed home."

"Anybody at Trèves you know, Lane?" asked Dexter.

The other nodded.

"I believe so. French army intelligence had word that—somebody was there."

F.A.I. sent word later in the day that Prince Adolph of Karlsruhe would visit the headquarters of Von Gallwitz's army for lunch, and Lane went over with a tray of bombs and a sickening sense of coming failure in his heart.

Between Trèves and Metz he met a solitary German airman and made no effort to avoid him. Lane was a sharp and daring fighter and a brilliant airman and he was flying a fast Curtiss. The German, though solitary and unsupported, swerved to gain the sun, but Lane went parallel and took the upper position first. He dived with the sun at his back and got in two bursts at fifty yards, but his opponent side-slipped and flew to the flank of his attacker. Lane stalled and fell back on his tail, but the other man dropped as quickly, banked round, and fired as he turned.

Lane straightened his machine, shut off his engines, and glided down. He wanted to die on the ground, and with every sobbing breath he drew his heart cried out against the injustice of this sudden ending to his quest.

His wheels touched the ground lightly and the machine ran smoothly over the stubble of a newly reaped field. He pulled feebly at the strap which bound him to his seat, and then his head fell forward and the light of day went out.

When he recovered consciousness he was lying on his back, a folded coat was supporting his head, and he had a drowsy sense of comfort. He opened his eyes slowly.

An officer was kneeling at his side, and some German soldiers were grouped at a respectful distance.

The officer was a man of fifty, clean cut of face and very gray about the temples. This Lane saw as in a dream. He knew that this man had shot him down and felt no sense of resentment. It was fair, but, oh, if he had had another day—a few more hours!

"I am afraid you are in a bad way, my friend," said a gentle voice. "You have no identity badge on your wrist. Will you tell me your name?"

"Lane—Ace High."

"Lane?" There was distress in the officer's voice. "Lane of the Ace High? Incredible!"

Lane closed his eyes. He knew he was dying and he was at peace, only an uneasy sense of work left undone troubled the serenity of his soul. And the officer was speaking:

"I am sorry. I know all about you. My mother told me. I am Prince Kurt of Wennigen. You have heard of me?"

Lane nodded. All the army had heard of the fifty-year-old airman and his singlehanded victories. Kurt bent down his eagle face and spoke slowly and deliberately into the American's ear, and Lane nodded and smiled and smiling, died.

Prince Adolph lunched with the staff of Von Gallwitz's army, but his cousin, Kurt of Wennigen, came too late for the meal, but in time for the coffee.

"This morning," said Kurt, as they sat under the great elms of the Château Framlis, a gay group of staff officers which included Adolph, greatly relieved by the courteous greeting he had received from his cousin, "this morning, I fought with an American hero."

Adolph caught his eye and laughed. His laugh meant nothing but polite evidence of his interest.

"Your highness laughs," said Kurt easily. "Perhaps your highness doubts my word?"

It may have been his fourth liqueur which blunted Adolph's sensitive instinct for danger.

"I certainly doubt your word, my dear friend, when you tell me that an American—"

Kurt flung the contents of his coffee cup straight at the smiling face.

"It is unpardonable to doubt the word of a Wennigen," he said.

That evening, in the tactful absence of the general and his staff, they fought the matter out in the rosery of the Château, and Kurt killed his man at the fourth pass.

He wiped his sword and delivered himself to custody. To the officer of the guard he made this request:

"Will you be so good as to wire to her highness, the grand duchess, and tell her that the affair of Fräulein Lexington is satisfactorily ended?"

CHAPTER IV

HOOKY WHO PLAYED WITH GERMANS

The Companions of the Ace High shared few of the joyous illusions which were held by their fellow airmen. There were enthusiastic American, British and French flyers who babbled of the sporting spirit which Fritz showed in the air, of what a good fighter he was and how excellently chivalrous.

Members of the Umpteenth British squadron were dining with the Ace High one night and one of the Britishers was expatiating upon the chivalric trait in the German airman's character.

"Fritz is impossible on the ground," he said, "but upstairs he's a little gentleman."

"Sure," said Dexter, "sure he is; by the way, when did he bomb your hospitals last?"

Whereupon the Britisher was dumb.

Beckworth of the Americans took up the mangled cause one afternoon when he had literally dropped in to tea.

"I'll say this for Heinie," he said, "that in the air he's fine."

"I guess he comes down to sleep sometimes," said the skeptical Dexter, "and a lot of that fineness wears off. How many kiddies were killed when he raided Paris last week and dropped his eggs on soldiers' orphanages?"

Of all the companions, only Hooky Patterson remained loyal to the tradition of German knight-errantry.

"There's something about the airman that's different," he insisted. "He's a good little sport and he'll put up a fight if he has a ghost of a chance of pulling through."

"A rat will do that," said the dampening Dexter. "It's the man who puts up a fight when there's no chance—who'll fight a losing battle and knowing he's losing, fights all the better—who's my sportsman. Hooky, I've said before and I'm saying again, that there are Germans and Germans, and with the exception of Prince Kurt they're all Germans.

"And I guess it was only an exaggerated view of the—no, I won't say it. Maybe Kurt is white, and there's always a chance that he swapped cradles at birth with the infant child of Bridget the cook. I read a story like that somewhere."

Hooky was not convinced. It was one of his weaknesses that he liked "playing with Germans."

No individual airman, except perhaps Vedrines, the French ace, landed so frequently in the forbidden land as he. Hooky had, to his credit an evening spent in a Munich movie theater, dressed in full uniform, be it added.

It was Hooky who had given an aerial performance for the benefit of a Nuremburg children's school picnic and botanical ramble, and had been vociferously "hoched" by the studious but misguided young folk of Bavaria until the performance had been interrupted by the arrival of a flight of German machines and a short sharp dog fight which had crippled one of his enemies and had forced down another.

"Your tastes are low," said Dexter when told of the occurrence, "and you were wasting good petrol. Providentially you strafed a machine, but what startling information did you gather from your reconnaissance?"

Whereupon Hooky spoke surprisingly of troop trains moving toward the Tirol, of great road convoys bound in the same direction; of an immense bombing flight he had observed in the distance also headed for Innsbruck.

"Why didn't you tell me that at first?" demanded Dexter wrathfully. "That means an attack upon our blessed Italian allies and incidentally upon the republic of San Romino."

"It never struck me that that was important," said Hooky in all innocence, "but I'll tell you, O King, what I did see. Between Ostenburg and Dweiplatz there's the loveliest rose garden ever. Say, I smelled 'em five thousand up—like as if the jars of glory had been uncovered to the sound of the fiddles—and I just went down and gloated."

"You want a tonic," said Dexter wearily. "Go over the Badische Soda-Fabrik at Mannheim and have a good pull at the poison gas they turn out from that village."

"Anyway," persisted Hooky stoutly, "I speak of Fritz as I find him—he's a hog, but he has his points."

"So has every hog," said Dexter, waving the champion of Kultur from his presence. "Go play, Hooky, and take all tomorrow for getting better acquainted with your little friends."

The next afternoon the gossip of the good Bürger of Zweiburg who were gathered about the three tables of the beer hall was interrupted by a solemn white-faced man.

"There is a so-high airplane above the village," he said, "and Mr. Sanitary Inspector Blomhof believes that it is the airplane of the enemy."

In these simple words was it announced that war had come to the pastoral people of Zweiburg.

They crowded into the street and shaded their eyes.

High in the blue gamboled a tiny white-winged scout. It looped and windmilled, dived and climbed and presently the "who-o-o" of its engines ceased and it glided down.

"A star is on the wing," said the host of the Golden Lion, and his voice was tremulous, "therefore it is true, as I have so long insisted—American soldiers are in France."

There was a tense silence.

"If he should drop a Bombe?" said a voice.

Pilot Hooky Patterson looked down and saw the crowd scatter.

"This comes of cutting your nails on Sunday," he said bitterly. "I knew I oughter brought a bomb!"

He glided in a circle over the red roofs, admired the old stone bridge across the little mountain stream— he came down to 50 feet to identify the period of the architecture—then, putting in his engine, he zoomed up, leaving behind him ample material for local history. For from that day forward all events in Zweiburg dated from the day of the so-unexpected American airman.

Hooky was happy, for the day was bright, the sky was cloudless, and he was pursuing what his chief called an "irresponsible reconnaissance." By a contrivance of his own he was carrying five hours' fuel and he had three hours to go. Therefore, when he came to a wild, wide stretch of moorland bisected by a long white road he decided to make a landing.

He chose a place where cows were grazing near a farmhouse—the one building in sight for miles. Long before he reached his landing place he throttled back his engine so that there was nothing remarkable in the fact that his arrival did not seem to invite the attention or excite the interest of the unknown farmer.

The meadow on which he descended was wide and sufficiently screened from the road for his purpose. He unstrapped himself, took two long-barreled revolvers from their sheaths in the fuselage and jumped to the ground.

He had no exact plan save to pursue inquiries, and as to what those inquiries would be, he had only the vaguest notion, for he was 200 miles from the nearest fighting front and away from the main communications.

But Hooky realized virtuously that he was on reconnaissance, and he had that curious faith in the potentialities of the commonplace which is the moral standby of every space reporter. Only the space reporter does not pack two guns, nor has he a one-hundred-and-twenty-horse-power Liberty Scout to make his getaway if his subject proves restive.

Hooky Patterson jumped the low fence of the farmhouse with a certain confidence. He was approaching the building from its blank end. He made his way cautiously to what he judged to be the rear of the premises, that face which was turned away from the road. There was not a soul in sight. There was not even a living thing visible, a fact which occurred to him as being strange.

No geese quacked or hens clucked in startled fright. He saw a kennel, but the dog was gone. There was a big low door near the end of the building on this side, and it stood open. Boldly he walked into the big, flagged kitchen, but it was empty. The embers of a fire glowed on the hearth, the table was laid with a red-and-white checkered tablecloth, and by the side of the fire some garments of feminine wear were hanging over the back of a high chair.

"Who's in the house?" he called, and his voice echoed hollowly. He tried one of the two doors leading from the room and it opened with difficulty, for there was some sort of pressure being exercised from the other side. Hooky put his broad shoulder to the door and pushed, and the door gave reluctantly because a dead man had been sitting against it and was now lying sideways athwart.

Hooky stepped over the body after a swift glance. Without taking any detailed note he realized that the room was in disorder, that drawers were open and books, papers and odds and ends of clothing were scattered over the floor.

What interested him most was that the man behind the door had his throat cut, and through the opposite door which led to a bedroom, he could see two shod feet with the toes upturned significantly. It was a girl of eighteen and she was dead.

Hooky stared pitiably down at the pinched white face for a second and resumed his search. The dog he found before the house, clubbed to death. An old man, who had evidently been one the farm hands, lay under a broken down cart.

He stooped and touched the body, It was still warm. He had not a great deal of experience in murders, but calculated that the crime had been committed three or four hours before arrival.

Such was the inborn respect for that intangible thing, "the law," that his first inclination was to fly to the nearest town and report the happening.

This impulse he checked and came into the sunlight holding his leather helmet under his arm the better to scratch his head, which seemed the only appropriate action in so extraordinary a situation.

He was more than a little shocked: he whose steel-gray eye had flashed over gun sights and whose brain and hand in perfect unison had sent a score of men to their deaths. It was an outrageous, bewildering happening, an illegality which showed black amidst the murky lawlessness of war.

There was nobody in sight on the long stretch of road, and he walked slowly back to the field where he had left his machine. The propeller was turning slowly—he had not stopped the engine—and he lifted the tail so that the plane faced right for a climb, and he was hoisting himself into the fuselage when a familiar sound reached his ear.

He stepped back to earth and shaded his eyes upward. Coming over was a German scout flying three or four hundred feet from the ground. The pilot had spotted the enemy machine and was swinging in a circle to confirm his first suspicion. Hooky pulled a big white handkerchief from the pocket of his leather jacket and waved it and after a while the nose of the German came down and he landed fifty yards from where Hooky stood.

A young man hoisted himself out, revolver in hand, the pair approaching each other warily.

"Put up your gun unless you want bloody war," cried Hooky in German. "I want a talk with you."

"Do you surrender?" asked the newcomer terribly.

"Do I look like surrendering?" demanded Hooky. "Put that gun away and don't be childish. I want to talk."

The German pilot was a tall young man, smartly uniformed and pardonably suspicious. He held his Mauser pistol in readiness and kept his eye on the long Colt which Hooky fondled in both hands.

"What do you want—you're English, yes?"

"American by birth, instinct and training," said Hooky. "Just stand where you are and I will explain just why I flagged you."

He told the discovery of his study and the German listened with interest. He shared his countrymen's fascination for the grotesque and frightful, and when Hooky had finished he thrust his pistol into his pocket and the two men tramped over to the farm.

They walked through the rooms, and the officer made a brief note in his pocketbook, entering punctiliously the hour and the position of the bodies.

"There has been an epidemic of these crimes," he said, "perpetrated by German soldier deserters. There are quite a number of these men about, especially in this part of the country. They hide in the woods and attack lonely farmhouses, usually by night. A crime of this character was committed only last

Sunday, twenty-five miles from here—probably this is the work of the same gang. Have you been through every room in the house?"

Hooky shook his head.

"I didn't go upstairs. I guess I was scared," he confessed.

The conversation had dropped into English, which his companion spoke with a good accent.

"Let, us go up," said the German, and mounted the steep stairs which led from the kitchen.

At the top of the stairs was a door fastened with a latch. Beyond this was a landing lit by a skylight which was evidently in the roof.

From the landing two doors opened. The first they tried was locked. The second was a storeroom and the door stood wide open. It had evidently been rifled. Shelves thick with dust showed round or square patches where packages had recently stood, and a big wooden box still half full of dried vegetables had been broken open.

They went back to the locked door.

"Anybody here?" asked Hooky, but his question brought no response.

"Break it open," said the German airman.

Hooky put his broad shoulders to the door and heaved. There was a moment of strain and then the door flew in with a crash.

A small window supplied light to the little bedroom in which they found themselves. At the first glance Hooky knew that this was not the type of bedroom he had seen downstairs. The bedstead was of brass and the linen of the disordered bed was finer. There was a satin-covered down quilt, and the pillows were frilled. The furniture too was good—the kind of furniture you would expect rather in a country chateau than in a wayside farm; and the floor was carpeted.

Everything in the room spoke of refinement and comfort. The arm chair at the foot of the bed was padded with morocco-covered cushions, the prints on the wall were engravings, well framed, and in a recess by the side of the bed were two rows of books.

The German who had introduced himself as Lieut. Baron von Thiesser was as much astonished as his companion.

"But what a room!" he exclaimed. "A woman's—look!"

Hung over the back of a chair was a blouse and a skirt and on another chair, neatly folded, were other articles of feminine wear.

But the room was apparently empty.

Hooky walked back to the door and examined the lock. It was turned and the key was on the inside. He walked across to the window. It was half opened, but fastened in that position by a staple, and evidently nobody could have passed through and replaced the staple.

By the side of the window on the opposite side of the room to that on which the bed was placed was a large clothes closet. Hooky pulled the door, but it was fast. He tried to turn the brass knob; it resisted, but resisted in such a way that left no doubt in his mind that somebody was holding it on the other side. Extending his strength he slowly turned the handle against his unseen opponent and jerked open the door. Then he stood back with a gasp of amazement.

Crouching in an attitude of terror on the floor of the little cupboard, clad in a dressing gown, was a girl. She raised her white face to the two men and stared with the bluest eyes Hooky had ever seen. A tangle of corn-gold hair streamed down her back, and the hands raised as if to ward off an expected blow were shapely and well tended.

"Well, what do you know about that!" demanded Hooky breathlessly, and stooping he lifted the girl to her feet.

Together the two men supported her to the armchair and she sank shaking and speechless into its depth.

She was still in a panic when told her story. She was the Gräfin von Salzmann, the daughter of the count of that name, and she came from Munich where she was attending an art school, and spent her summer holidays on this farm which was the property of her father. Here she painted and sketched.

Early that morning the farm been attacked by soldiers. She had seen them from her window and heard the struggle. They tried to break into her room but had been disturbed by the passage of an airplane.

"I passed over at 10 o'clock," the baron in explanation.

How long they had stayed or for how long they had been gone, she could not say. She had crouched for hours in the little closet, expecting to hear the splintering of the door.

They left her while she dressed and went down into the kitchen.

"The swine!" cried the Baron passionately. "The foul brutes! Himmel, if I had a so-disciplined platoon I'd rout them out of their woods—but we leave it to the police! The police! Criminals as bad!"

Hooky strolled to the door and again scrutinized the road. He at any rate had no desire to see a so-disciplined platoon goose-stepping his way, for he knew that not even the friendly intervention of a Baron von Theisser or a Countess von Salzmann would persuade the unchivalrous infantry of Germany to release him.

He walked back to the sitting room, exhilarated by the sense of adventure which only needed this suggestion of knight-errantry to give it a romantic completeness. He found the German pacing the flagged floor of the kitchen, his hands behind him, his chin upon his breast.

"I don't know how to—" began the Baron.

"Don't thank me," said Hooky. "Why, this is the sort of thing I am doing every day,"

The Baron did not complete his sentence, but continued his moody pacings. Presently they heard a step on the stairs and the girl descended to the room. She was still very white and looked from one man to the other, her gaze resting with unconquerable curiosity upon Hooky.

"This aviator is an American, who descended to make reconnaissance."

Her brows rose, and interest for the moment overcame her terror into which her experience had thrown her.

"I am greatly obliged to you," she said gravely. "And will you please let us go quickly? I am afraid that they will come back when Louis tells them I have money in the house."

"Louis?" asked the Baron.

She nodded.

"He was my boy servant. They took him with them when they went. I will show you."

She walked through the door and to the end of the house and pointed across the moor to a purple-shadowed wood two or three miles away.

"That is the way they went, I think," she said. "They were coming from that direction when I saw them. They took Louis away, and they will come back when he tells them I have money."

The two men looked at one another. How to get her away—that was the problem. Both men were flying in scouts, and there is no room for passengers, in these tiny machines, and at any rate it would have to be the German who made the offer, because it might be impossible for Hooky to land, and he had no desire to bring to the Ace High Airdrome such a charming souvenir of his "irresponsible reconnaissance."

Evidently the Baron was thinking on similar lines. Presently he said:

"If you will excuse me, I would like to speak to the gracious lady."

He drew her aside into the middle of the road and for a few moments they talked in a low voice. Presently he returned.

"There is a small town ten miles from here," he said. "I will fly there and send a car for the lady. In the meantime will you be so good as to stay with her until I return?"

"Sure," said Hooky heartily. "But, isn't there one of your airdromes near?"

The other shook his head.

"Not nearer than 60 miles," he said.

Again the Baron drew the girl aside and spoke to her. Presently he walked toward his machine and disappeared in the undergrowth, leaving the, girl and Hooky together. They heard the whirr of his engines and watched him zoom up and move swiftly northward. Then Hooky turned his attention to the girl.

He was not a lady's man and his supply of small talk was inconsiderable. He was, too, rather impressed by the fulfillment of healthy youth's dream, which is the rescue of damsels in distress under thrilling circumstances.

The girl was pretty, with a prettiness which is not unusual in certain parts of Prussia. If he was embarrassed, she at any rate was wholly self-possessed, and they talked on such safe subjects as perspective and color and avoided the war.

"Why, countess," said Hooky with enthusiasm, "all that art talk is easy for me. I am one of the grandest little artists that ever took a correspondent's course in painting in oils."

"Do you often come down to earth?" she asked with a smile.

"Nothing gives me greater pleasure than to play around with Hu—with bright-eyed children of the fatherland," he answered solemnly.

"I owe you a great deal," she said again, "I am sure—Look!"

He saw the horror in her eyes and followed the direction of her extended finger.

The moor on that side of the road where stood the farm was covered by light brush and heather. There were no bushes or trees to obstruct the view for miles, and coming toward them, knee-high in the undergrowth, were six men.

There was no need for Hooky to ask any questions. Two of the men still wore the round caps of the German Infantry and there was yet a trace of something that had been a uniform in their wild and varied apparel. They were less than a hundred yards when Hooky saw them, but they had evidently seen him and the girl long before she had detected their approach.

"The men—men—" she whispered, and clung trembling to his arm.

They came closer, and Hooky decided that this was the toughest bunch of citizens that it had ever been his misfortune to meet. Three of the men had rifles. The other three had service revolvers belted about their waists.

"Get into that bush behind me and lie down," said Hooky sharply, and when she obeyed he strolled forward to meet the party.

They halted at a dozen paces, the men with the rifles standing so that they covered him from their hips.

"What do you want?" he asked in German.

He had a feeling that any discussion was wholly gratuitous and unnecessary, a fact which was brought home to him a second later when two of the riflemen fired at him. The rifles went off like one. He leaped back to the cover of the bush and crouched down by the side of the girl.

"Run to my airplane," he said in English, "and lift the tail around so that the propellers are facing this way."

She slipped from his side and he heard the rustle of the bushes as she passed on her errand.

"Ping!"

A bullet zipped past his shoulder, and his Colt barked three times. He could just glimpse their movement and knew that they were spreading out to encircle him. He fired at one of the men as he crossed the road and saw him balance himself on one leg, absurdly like a ballet dancer, before he collapsed in a heap.

Then Hooky turned and dashed after the girl. She had swung the airplane round, and he noted that she carried a revolver, and nodded approvingly.

"Get what cover you can," he said, and jumped into the fuselage as his pursuers broke cover.

They came with a rush straight at the airplane before they realized what was happening. One of them saw the swing of the Vickers gun and shouted a warning. Before the men could throw themselves on their faces or spread for cover, Hooky's machine gun rattled. Two men went down, while the remainder crashed through the bushes. He sent a burst of fire after them and watched them as they blundered away toward the distant wood. Then he descended.

The revolver in the girl's hand was trembling when, for the second time that day, he lifted her to her feet.

"They've gone," he said cheerfully. She passed her trembling hand across her eyes and looked up at him gratefully.

"I knew they would come back," she said. "If you hadn't been here—"

He stopped her.

"Gracious lady," he said floridly, "if I hadn't been here I should have missed —a lot."

The last two words were spoken slowly and thoughtfully. They were spoken by a man who was not thinking of what he was saying, but whose every sense was concentrated in one and that the sense of hearing.

It was twenty-five minutes since the baron had left and, anyway, one airplane would not make that noise. He ran into the center of the clearing and looked upward. Coming from the north, in which direction the baron had gone, was not one, but twelve airplanes, and even at that distance Hooky's keen sight saw that the baron's little scout was leading the formation.

"Not an airdrome within sixty miles." he said grimly. "I guess this is where I go home."

The propeller was still turning slowly, and with a nod to the girl he stepped nimbly into the pilot's seat, adjusted and buckled the straps about his waist, and his hand was on the switch to open out the engine when a quiet voice at his side said:

"Come down, please."

He looked and gaped. The girl was no longer shaking, for a more holy emotion than fear possessed her, and the Mauser pistol which she was pointing straight at his body did not waver.

"It is forbidden that you should go," she said steadily. "The lieutenant told me I was not to allow you to depart."

"Is that so?" drawled Hooky, and put his engine full out.

The little scout jumped forward, increasing its momentum with every yard it covered. He did not hear the shots because the noise of the engines was too loud, but he felt the wind of the bullets as they passed him.

Up went the nose of his machine, and in something under sixty seconds he was a thousand feet above the earth. He judged his enemies to be at two thousand, and in rising he made a whole turn so that he was moving at right angles to the coming formation. The foremost of the machines dropped to the attack an maneuvered to get on his tail. They miscalculated the distance, and it was not until Hooky was flying at three thousand feet that the formation had secured its position again. Again the leader dived for him, but Hooky came around so that his nose met the attacker broadside. Two quick bursts in the center piece, and the enemy scout went down.

The second of the machines headed off and Hooky had time to make a brief survey of the field. He was now on the wing of the formation, and in the nearest machine be recognised the baron's scout. Straight for his enemy drove the American, his teeth set, his cold eyes fixed on his victim with the assurance of victory. The baron looped to avoid and get behind his attacker.

"Elementary," said Hooky, and shot him down in flames as the looping machine reached its zenith.

Some of the scouts were landing in the field he had left. He saw tiny figures gather about a tinier figure, which he judged was the girl, and swooped down upon the group. He saw them scatter and grinned.

As he cut off the engine for a glide he reached for a little dispatch bag that hung on the side of the fuselage, pulled his message pad toward him and wrote on his knees three words and these words were:

"Oh, you Hun!"

Over the group be dropped the bag with its streaming ribbons, and for the second time that day lamented the fate which brought him out without bombs.

"I rescued her; I saved her from death; I spoke to her, man to man, and she thanked me." said Hooky dismally, "and all the time she was framing it to get me pinched. Why, it's enough to shake a man's faith in humanity!"

"In Germans, you mean—why drag in humanity?" snarled Dexter.

CHAPTER V

HOOKY PATTERSON DIES ONCE

There was a man stretched on a long cane chair before the mess room of the Ace High. He sat with his elbows on the cane arms and his eyes were fixed on something that lay 10 miles beyond eternity.

This was the description of Pilot Hooky Patterson.

"Colonel," he said in perplexity, "Bertram rattles me; he never talks, he never laughs, he never admires the bright beauties of the perfect day or the soothing stillness of the starry night. He just sits next to ghosts and glooms stertorously. Why, that fellow's never nearer to earth than the Dog Star!"

Dexter filled the coffee cup and pushed it to his junior.

"Hooky," said he, "when you joined us we didn't agree to provide you with merry chatter. The Ace High is a peculiar institution and Bertram is a peculiar man. Suppose"—he took a cigar from his breast rocket, bit off the end with deliberation, and reached for the tiny silver lamps that stood on the table— "suppose you were a young Canadian who had been taken prisoner at Ypres."

"Duly supposed," said Hooky.

"And suppose you, being a fine, lusty lad, as you are, attracted the attention of the Herr Professor in charge of the new gas department—it was new at the time I am speaking about."

"The Herr Professor being at the front?"

"The Herr Professor being at the front," repeated Dexter, "and suppose that, instead of sending you away to a prison camp and reporting you in the usual way, you were kept a prisoner at the laboratory which the Herr Professor had established behind the German line, and from day to day he experimented on you—giving you first one kind of gas and then another. Not enough to kill, but enough to secure him certain data, pulse respiration, muscle contraction and other particulars—"

Hooky stared at him, shocked and pained.

"Good God! They didn't do that, did they?" he asked huskily.

"Do that? Is there anything out of Hell they wouldn't do? I tell you this and you can confirm it. They allowed an English officer to go untended with a broken rib till the rib gradually pierced the lung and then they took out the rib—without an anaesthetic! They have performed hundreds of amputations on prisoners without chloroform—hundreds! You don't know them, Hooky boy—you're playing with them. The men who set the code of the German Army were not men—"

He checked himself suddenly and his tense figure relaxed.

"Well, I'm telling you," he said in his old drawl, "that that greatly experimented-upon Canadian was friend Bertram. He escaped. Ever hear him cough?—queer, little, irritating cough. Do you know why his voice indoors is a shrill falsetto and out of doors a deep base? Gas, Hooky. The experiments of Herr Professor Zonnendorp."

"Good God!" whispered Hooky, staring blankly out of the window.

Dexter rose.

"A grand aggregation of aerial talent will parade tomorrow morning," he said with his old flippancy, "and will visit Boulay, wind and weather permitting. You are cast for a part—deputy assistant marshal of the parade. In other words, Hooky, you will be on escort duty to a Franco-British bombing squadron which is due over Germany somewhere about noon."

"Huh!" said Hooky gloomily, for he loved not to be one of a crowd.

"Colonel," Hooky's voice was worried; "there's one thing I'd like to say about the Ace High. Of course, I know everybody has a personal grievance against Fritz except me. I know that the work is—peculiar. All that I know. The fellows are fine and the work is fine and it's all candy to me, but I got that out-of-it feeling. I'm in the squadron and everybody's lovely to me, but—well, somehow. I feel they don't speak my language, Colonel."

Dexter nodded slowly.

"That's so, Hooky. I guess I know just how you feel. But, Hooky, don't you realize that you are dealing with men who have died once?"

"Died once?"

"Some of 'em have died twice—their hearts have all gone shrively and their hopes have dried up like raindrops dry on a hot stove. They've died once, Hooky, carried their despair to a hell of their own and come back to the world looking at things from a new angle."

Hooky dropped his eyes.

"Why, then," his laugh was a little helpless, "they must just hate me; I'm raw ignorant, Colonel, and—and—it never struck me that way before. If dying once means taking a big chance of death, something outside the ordinary chances, why, let me have an opportunity."

"I certainly will," said Dexter.

On the following afternoon, "the intrepid leader of our chasing squadron"—to quote an official description of Oberleutnant Gloebe—"came swiftly from cloudy cover to attack a solitary scout which was buzzing homeward at sunset."

The pilot of that scout was Hooky Patterson, and he feared neither man nor Hun. He recognized the imminence of the danger, but it was the other fellow's danger that appealed to him.

As Lieut. Gloebe hurtled downward, both guns going furiously, Hooky performed the one trick which the German Air Service have taught their rivals. It is called, after the dead airman, "the Immelmann."

Up shot the nose of the scout as though to climb. Before it reached a stall Hooky jammed over the rudder sharp and the head of the machine fell leftward. It was a lightning turn which brought his nose where his tail had been.

The attacker rolled to avoid the shower of nickel that was coming his way.

"Of the dead speak nothing but good," said Hooky, and threw two quick bursts at his assailant.

The intrepid leader of our chasing squadron fell, emitting smoke and flame to advertise his uneasiness. Hooky would have dropped behind him, but his conscience was pricking him. He had been sent to cover a bombing raid on enemy hangars and had found the work too dull for a young man with a temperament, and had conveniently lost himself in a cloud ball and had played hooky, as was his wont.

He had swooped joyously down toward a column of infantry upon the march and had machine-gunned them to confusion and had returned via Ypres in time to mix himself up in a great dog fight between the Umpteenth British and the 33rd German Squadrons. It wasn't his fight, really, and he knew nothing of the furious feud between the Umpteenth and 33rd—a feud which had its beginning in the dark ages of the war—but the fight looked good to him and he dropped into it in time for the final mixing which covered the Flanders landscape with airplane souvenirs.

He dipped into the airdrome in the most staid and regulation fashion. Ordinarily his landing was distinguished by stunts and once he had come in upside down and narrowly escaped an early dissolution. But he felt that the occasion demanded propriety and respectability. Something with a hint of old age and settling down.

So he came home primly; descended with dignity and spoke gentle words to the mechanics.

Dexter, commandant and tyrant of the squadron, he saw out of the corner of his eye, and endeavored to avoid him; but Dexter was a difficult man to avoid.

"Why, it's Hooky!" he said with an extravagant air of surprise, "and how did you leave Boulay airdrome?"

"Boulay, sir," he blinked rapidly, a sure sign of embarrassment. "Ah, Boulay—picture to yourself, Colonel, a wild tangle of woodland and lake, with here and there a golden quadrilateral of unharvested grain to break the illusion of virgin land. Picture little clusters of red roofs standing vividly against the white chalk quarries, the whole bathed in a soft radiance—" He stopped and asked anxiously, "How does that go, colonel?"

"It doesn't go at all, Hooky. You're certainly strong on word painting, but I'd rather you gave me a brief and pretty little essay on discipline and duty in relation to aerial scouting."

"I never was strong on that textbook stuff," said Hooky. "Now I'm going to be a brave little man and own up. I had a look at Boulay and I sort of inspected the bombing gentlemen and it looked kind of a yawn to me.

"Like one of those dissipated evenings you have with Aunt Jane in the best parlor—out with the checkerboard and away with melancholy. You know! So I went along with a French fellow as far as Douai. I guess he was taking photographs, for he just smooched around and did nothing for the communiqués.

"Then I met an English fellow who was going some on a Bristol fighter and I pulled out with him till he did nothing, too, an then I sort of loafed around laying eggs and I butted into what appeared to be a regrettable occurrence over Ypres, and then—why, then I came home, colonel."

Dexter surveyed him with a hard blue eye.

"Did you see anything which might be of the slightest interest to Mr. Pershing or Mr. Haig or Mr. Foch or any of the gentlemen who are running this war?" he asked, and Hooky shook his dismal face.

"Nothing, colonel—not a blamed thing. There's a German attack developing behind Menin, but I suppose they know all about that. The Hun is building a new defense line between Valenciennes and the Belgian frontier—they were camouflaging it as I came over. There are new airdromes east-northeast of Valenciennes, and the headquarters of the 23th German Army has been shifted to Hirson."

Dexter gasped.

He had a tab on all Military Intelligence knew, and none of these things were known.

"How did you find out—about the 29th?" he demanded.

"I asked a German soldier," said Hooky simply. "You see, I went down and had a look around—met a soldier— a most engaging man named Fritz, who wanted to desert and cross to our lines and asked me to give him a lift. He used to write poetry for the Jugend—a most intelligent person—"

"Keep the rest for your book," said Dexter, cutting short the narrative, "and attend to me. Bertram is going over Lille tonight and maybe elsewhere. It is a special job, and the Huns will take extra special precautions. He goes with one scout as escort and you're that scout."

Hooky nodded.

"Colonel—" he began.

"Let me finish," said Dexter seriously; "If you play hooky, you leave Bertram flat and I'm just telling you this: keep by your man till he's through or dead. If that desire for roving seizes you and you leave him, why, Hooky, you can make your landing in another airdrome."

Hooky saluted and went grimly forth.

That night, in the darkness of the airdrome, he met his man.

"Sorry to bring you out on this trip," said Bertram in a voice which alternately boomed and squeaked, "and I might as well tell you right here that I'm not sure whether our adventure will end pleasantly."

"Anything you say to cheer me up is appreciated, sir and friend," said Hooky earnestly. "Any bright little morsel of encouragement that comes to your lips, why, let her trip."

Bertram laughed softly, but his laugh ended in a dry, rasping cough.

"Sorry," he apologized. "I was gassed, you know. But don't think I'm being funny—I think we may have a bad time. We've got five minutes, and I'll tell you what I'm after. There's a scientist attached to the 12th German army, a gentleman and a scholar named Zonnendorp—friend of mine. He used to be chief stoker of the gas works, but now he's running lights."

"Searchlights?"

"Searchlights—the scientific side. He's an authority on refraction and optics and all that sort of thing, and gas was really only a side line. Funny looking old fellow with a gray beard. He has invented a new lamp—throws a strong blue beam—and he is somewhere in the neighborhood of Lille."

"I've been out after him for three weeks. It was dead easy to pick up the light after Intelligence discovered what was going on. He's dodged me—his apparatus is on a railway truck and he can move from Lille to Metz and from Metz to Mulhausen in a day. But now he's in the Lille area. A prisoner taken by the British gives us the tip."

"What do I do?" asked Hooky.

"Stand by to strafe the fighting planes—he puts them up to guard the light, which is a pretty important invention. It can pick up a plane on a moonlight night, and that takes some doing. He knows I'm after him, too, and that makes him careful. I'll bomb the light and you keep off the chasers—that's all there is to it. If I fail, get down to the light and use your machine gun. Watch my signals and jump in quick when I give the word."

Once they saw the ghostly blue flame of an exhaust which advertised the presence of a German night flyer and Hooky put over his controls mechanically and was shaping for attack when he remembered his chief's injunctions and came back to course with a sniff of self-pity.

The green light flickered and went out, which either meant that the bomber had smelled scouts above him or that his battery had failed. Hooky lost height and tapped a lamp signal: "Can't see you."

Almost immediately the bomber's green lamp winked twice and went out. Hooky strained his eyes left and right, above and below. There was no sign of hostile craft. He keyed: "Where?" And this time the green lamp stuttered at length: "Under me. Four scouts following my exhaust."

Hooky tested his gun, throttled back his engine, and began gliding. He reached the bomber's level and looked down. Against the blackness of the earth there was no sign of airplane, which was not remarkable, for night flying machines are painted dead black.

He switched his engines on and fell sideways, flattened and turned almost in one motion, and saw plain against the starry skies the outline of a German scout. It was just a little above him and about 200 yards distant. He opened out full and climbed, keeping his enemy in sight. At the right height he swung and dived.

"Ticka-ticka-ticka-ticka!"

The German machine dropped like a rabbit to its bolt.

Hooky fell in behind his bomber. The flare of the exhaust was safe, and if the enemy could follow the ghost-blue flag of flame, so could he. He lost all sense of direction; his eyes glued to the fluttering exhaust, he followed blindly, content only to keep his place in this "formation" of two.

Presently Bertram moved round and Hooky conformed to the movement. The enemy was going to be a very tame one, but he had a virtuous sense of duty faithfully performed. Now, by the swinging compass card, he knew that he was homing, and he wondered whether there would be anybody at home to play billiards with him.

It occurred to him that it was a fool idea, anyway, to escort a night bomber. The Hun never attacked in the air at night; yet he remembered with a start that four scouts had undoubtedly followed Bertram. He had climbed after the bomber turned homeward and was now guided by the green light which showed steadily. Over Lille it winked with great rapidity and Hooky spelled the message:

"Hang around there."

Hooky blinked through his goggles at the astonishing order, and his Lucas lamp snapped furiously with sarcasm:

"Where do I find the hook?"

The green light was gone. He could see the bomber circling widely over the silent town and himself made a wider circle, keeping his convoy on the inside. He examined his petrol gauge. He was good for another hour's flying, and, if necessary, he could land in any of the innumerable British airdromes to be found in this part of France.

But the enterprise was tedious to one of his temperament.

Then Bertram signaled:

"Light here."

Hooky looked down, but could see nothing save the faintest flicker of yellow light. This went out and the ground was black again. Then into the skies there leaped a blue-white bar of light. It was stationary for the space of 30 seconds, then it began to move slowly in the direction of his restricted orbit.

He throttled back his engine and glided under the light bar, turned inward, toward the place where the searchlight stood, and climbed again. Momentarily he had lost sight of Bertram, but reaching his old level he could see the occasional twinkle of the green light. Then, most unexpectedly, the straight beam began to spread until It was a broad, luminous funnel and through its center ran one slim rod of light, intensely blue.

The edge of the funnel caught Bertram's machine just as a bursting fire bubble to the left of the searchlight told Hooky that the first bomb had been dropped. Bertram slid sideways, but the light held him, and Hooky made a swift scrutiny of the skies for a sign of the enemy scouts which his companion had promised.

Now the guns were going. They flickered and flashed from a dozen points in the void, and in the inexorable beams of the light they burst black and white about the struggling bomber. Bertram had turned and was dipping straight for the light, when a high-explosive shell burst under his tail and blew away his elevator.

Hooky could only stand by helplessly and watch the bomber fall into that slow spin from which nothing but the fates of machines can emerge. Down—down—down the light followed the lamed bomber, and if light may show emotion, this malignant cold beam was gloating.

Hooky spun round for direction and dropped at an angle of 55 degrees. Straight for the light he dived. For the fraction of a second he was in the beam passing his falling friend: then, with both guns roaring, he pulled himself out of the dive, and, skimming the ground, drove under the beam and straight at the lamp. The beam dropped. Straight in his eyes fell the blinding glare, which brought him so acute a pain that he closed them tight and dropped his head.

For a fraction of a second that light penetrated through his lids and, as it seemed, his very skull, then came blackness He opened his eyes to find the skies a pale green waste filled with round purple disks that floated left and right, up and down, whichever way he looked.

He closed his eyes tight to rid the retina of this weird optical illusion and zoomed up. There was no light showing on the ground, and he picked up his course from the stars. Half an hour as later his Very light was burning over a British airdrome, and he was descending.

"Sorry to trouble you, but I've run out of juice and would one of your fellows lend me a pair of antiglare goggles?" he demanded of the officer on duty.

"Strafing searchlights?" asked the officer sympathetically. "By the way, did you see their new patent blinder?"

"I saw it all right," said Hooky grimly.

The British riggers made an inspection of his machine and passed it sound, and back into the night sky came Hooky praying his chance. He was over Aubers when the light shot up again and he dropped to a low level. It was dangerous work, for the ground hereabouts is covered with tall chimney stacks.

The visibility was fairly good, and beyond one narrow squeak where he had to make a vertical bank to escape a gaunt column of brickwork, he met with no adventure. The light was groping about the skies as though in search of something. That something was a German scout flying at 18,000 feet and Hooky saw the elusive glitter of it when the beam caught its black wings.

He adjusted his goggles and climbed a little. At the proper distance he dived again with both his machine guns going. At a distance of 50 yards the lamp went out, but Hooky kept his guns working until he was well past. He slipped on two more trays of ammunition and came round on an almost flat turn. As he did so the light leaped up again.

So he had not succeeded.

He set his teeth and this time came at it sideways. You can strafe a light as well through the projector as through its lens—and this lamp undoubtedly had a lens. This time he came lower and he knew that his bursts were near. The light went out before he came to it, flashed up again as though in mockery when he had passed.

He had the uneasy conviction that they wanted him to fire, that those unseen men were fooling him. He took from a canvas locker a small parachute flare, climbed a little and fired it. As the magnesium burst into blinding light he came and dived—and saw.

A box car, steel protected—he guessed—with steel shutters to protect the lamp within.

He was not 20 yards from the ground, and the parachute flare made all things within the radius of its illumination as clear as though they were in the light of day.

Before the superstructure which housed the light was a narrow platform which was guarded by a small rail. It had evidently been a conductor's brake van until converted to military use. A seat of some sort had been placed on the platform and in that seat was a man, his wrists fastened to the railing. The shutter which hid the light was just above his head.

Hooky saw it all in a flash, saw the droop of the figure, the big dark patch on the man's front where his machine-gun bullets had struck.

"Bertram!" said Hooky softly. "Bertram! They put him there so that anybody strafing the light— Bertram—and I've killed him!"

His brain worked like the slats of a blind, he swooned and recovered consciousness in fractions of a second. Mechanically he was climbing, mechanically he saw the hideous light flash up again and brought his scout round to attack. He was not enraged; he was not even sorry. He was just petrified—the very functions of thought were damned.

"Bertram—they fixed him there—and I've murdered him," he said wonderingly.

He repeated the fact to himself, yet could not realize all that the words meant. His mind was dead; yes, that was it! He had died once, as Dexter said he must. He had died of horror. All the good pleasantness of life had been burned off and left him desolate, without even the consolation of self-pity.

Again the light was following the high scout and Hooky changed direction. He set himself to a steady climb and in 35 minutes he was at the requisite height. And then the light went out and the scout vanished. Hooky peered around for the sign of an exhaust, but without success.

He dropped down again, hoping to pick up the box car. Then he started, for he had seen for a moment the incautious flare from a firebox near to where the car stood.

They were coupling an engine to it. Presently he saw the intermittent gleam of the engine fire as it pulled through Lille and take the Mesières road.

"From Lille to Metz," repeated Hooky, thoughtfully.

He followed, having no plans, yet dreading to lose sight of the tiny speck of smooth moving light which marked the target of his hate. .

Over Orchies he sighted two large exhausts and they were moving toward Condé.

"Handley-Pages," he noted numbly, and climbed to avoid them, for Handley-Pages on their midnight journeys are tetchy and unsociable things and liable to snap, for they carry four bored machine gunners, only too anxious for practice.

A thought—an inspiration came to Hooky.

His signal lamp fluttered urgently and presently a tiny star quivered in the skies.

"Mark train on your right front," tapped Hooky.

A pause, then—

"Seen," blinked the star; "who are you?"

Hooky gave a code word and a number, and unseen airmen replied:

"Wts mtter wi trn?"

Hooky's fingers trembled as he tapped:

"Carries inventr poison gas."

A longer pause.

"Absltly."

A shorter pause.

"Thks: Go on: Sn gd trgt."

The latter sentence was evidently for the bomber companion. Hooky saw a blue exhaust turn and make for the railway, and followed so close in its wake that the monstrous shape grew visible against the heavens.

On the outskirts of Valenciennes, the big bomber dived.

The first bomb fell before the train, burst, and in its red glare showed the ruin it wrought: the second bomb fell on the first two cars behind the engine.

No need to doubt the completeness of the work. The wreckage glowed redly and burst into flame, and the Handley-Page swung majestically back to her course, winking illiterately:

"It dd hm no gd! Thnks fr drwg attentn. Gd by."

Hooky came lower, circling about the wreck. He waited until the bomber was well away and dropped his last magnesium flare.

One man was staggering along the permanent way, stumbling blindly through the darkness. He looked up as the flare burst into light, and Hooky saw a man with a short gray beard. At the sight of him his arrested rage and grief and horror broke bounds.

"Damn you!" he yelled, and his guns went for the last time that night.

Dexter was waiting for his return and saw the look on the boy's face.

"Bertram's dead," he jerked harshly, "I killed him. They tied him to the light and I machine-gunned him."

Dexter said nothing, and Hooky stood nervously twisting his fur gloves, his mouth working.

"I got the Professor," he said, and burst into a fit of sobbing.

Dexter tiptoed out of the deserted mess room.

CHAPTER VI

THE MAN WHO SHELLED OPEN BOATS

The name "Stanford I. Severs" written on the southeast corner of a check was never good for much more than a few hundred dollars. He was not the kind of man to let his money lay idle, and he never had a great deal of money, anyway. He was a bachelor, a little fussy, a little old fashioned.

He had a fox terrier, played golf twice a week at the country club and lived in one of those handsome colonial houses which are shipped to you in a sealed box-car for $5000, and which may be erected by any man with a smattering of architecture and a taste for bricklaying between Saturday and Monday.

Only Stanford Seyers' house looked just like the magazine advertisement, and its interior was even an improvement upon the catalogue. He lived with his mother—a placid and, in consequence, a somewhat selfish life.

His income more than sufficed for his needs; he contributed to the funds of the church, and took an interest in the work of the Boys' Social Club. A sandy-haired man of 30, slightly bald, thin and middle-sized, you might pass him on the street a score of times and never remember that you had seen him at all.

His mother was the average American mother, which means that she had shrewdness, a sense of humor, and a wider interest in affairs than her son. She was in Morocco when the war broke out, on a summer vacation.

That would sound wildly improbable to the average Englishman or Frenchman, to whose mothers a journey to Harrogate or Paris-Plage is a wild and lonesome adventure, but in prewar days Europe knew that independent American mother, and the couriers, guides and dragomans of 29 nations will testify to her energy.

Yet independence and self-confidence have their limitations. She was in England for 13 months before she ventured on the return voyage. Stanford came over to bring her back and they sailed in the good ship Aramac.

Three days out came a torpedo, but the passengers had leisure to take to the boats. The sea was calm, the weather was fair and the day was warm. There were patrol vessels in the neighborhood, so there was really no very great danger.

Mrs. Seyers behaved with the most admirable courage in the face of danger, and was joking with her more perturbed son when the submarine came to the surface 400 yards away and began shelling the open boats. He fired half a dozen shells before a smudge of smoke on the horizon sent him diving, but those six shots were more than sufficient to rearrange the life of Stanford I. Seyers.

The first shot killed his mother—not nicely, as women are killed in stories, but so that after the shell burst he never saw the mother he knew and loved. Only a shapeless something that sprawled across the gunwale. And at the sight of the horror a pretty, fair-haired woman who was crouching in the bow of the boat had suddenly gone mad. Her shrieking laughter remained with Stanford, so that at the sound of laughter thereafter he shook from head to foot.

Until then, like many of his countrymen, he had only taken a detached interest in a war which had already lasted too long. Thereafter the war became his personal affair. He went back to New Jersey, settled his affairs, sold his house, and when his business was done took the first boat for Le Havre.

Among his fellow passengers was a gray man who wore the uniform of the French air service and the distinctive badge which marked him as an "Ace of Aces," which meant that he had destroyed more than his share of flying Germans.

Stanford, who had developed a passion for solitude, and who had no other desire in the world save to reach Europe and kill Germans, and no other fear but that by some miracle the war would end before he received the necessary authority to begin his work, neither sought nor avoided the French officer, who, to do him justice, exhibited the same wish for solitude as Stanford.

One day he discovered his French officer was an American, and a steward volunteered the gratuitous information that his name was Dexter and that he was a millionaire cattleman who had made a fortune in the Argentine. Stanford dimly remembered that in reading the numerous articles which had appeared in print on the sinking of the Aramac the name Dexter had appeared.

The two men spoke for the first time when they were two days from the British Coast. They were leaning over the rail in their life belts watching the flicker of gun flashes on the eastern horizon, where American and British destroyers were dealing with a submarine which had made two attempts to torpedo their boat that evening.

Stanford watched intently, his hands clasped, his eyes straining to give shape to the distant ships of war. He was oblivious of the other's presence, then—

"Damn them!" he muttered.

"Amen!" said the man at his side.

Stanford glanced round curiously and saw that it was the man called Dexter, who was chewing an unlighted cigar. There was a silence which lasted for five minutes before Dexter spoke:

"Ever been torpedoed?"

"Once," said Stanford shortly.

"H'm!"

Another long silence.

"Lose—anybody?" jerked Dexter.

Stanford resented the question. It was a subject on which he could not speak, but something in the man's voice asked for his confidence.

"Mother," he said gruffly.

Another period of silence. The gun flashes were no longer seen. A green rocket curved slowly from the horizon and broke into a splutter of white balls.

"They've got her." said Dexter exultantly. "I hate to ask you questions, but it is not idle curiosity. "Were you on board the Aramac when she sank?"

"Yes."

"Did—did they shell your boat?"

The other nodded.

"And is that where—where it happened?"

"That's where it happened," repeated Stanford. "It was awful—awful." He shuddered. "I can't bear to think of it—a woman went mad—"

He heard the catch of his companion's breath, and stopped.

"What are you going to do?" asked Dexter after a while.

"I guess I'm going to get even, some way," said Stanford, his voice shaking with passion. "Somebody's got to pay for that. If God lets me live till I have killed one German, I ask no more."

Dexter turned and laid his hand on the other's shoulder.

"I'm going back to form a new flying squadron," he said, quietly. "You can join me."

"Flying?" Stanford stared at him in the growing darkness. "But I've never thought of flying. I guess I am not cut out for that."

"Join with me," said Dexter again. "I've got a lot of old scores to settle, too. I left France a month ago to take my wife back to America."

"Your wife?"

"My wife," repeated the other quietly. "She was the woman who went mad."

It was 16 months after Stanford Seyers became a member of the Ace High Squadron and nine months after he had killed his first man, the redoubtable Capt. Baron von Seidlitz of the 67th Chasing Squadron, that Dexter spoke again of the sinking of the Aramac. From that night when the two men had spoken on the deck of the homeward-bound French mail to the sunny afternoon when Dexter had summoned Pilot Seyers to his bureau no word had passed between them on the subject. Stanford had gone about his work, co-operating with his fellows, helping in the settlement of innumerable little vendettas, bombing, fighting, reconnoitering, whatever was the task assigned to him on the daily routine which was pinned to the green baize board in the mess room.

He came to Dexter's bureau, a little leaner, a little harder and a little older than he had been in the days when life ran smoothly and his greatest ambition was to raise American beauties in his tiny rosery.

"Sit down, Stanford," said Dexter. He was known as Stanford in the squadron and had taken his commission in that name. "Help yourself to the cigars. I haven't had a chat with you for a long time. I guess you haven't forgotten the Aramac, and neither have I. I think we can continue the little conversation we began some time ago. Do you know the name of the U-boat commander?'

"Yes," replied the other quietly. "Lieut. Capt. Casselmann."

"Right." nodded Dexter. "I see you have been pursuing inquiries."

"It was in the newspapers," said the other; "but two names were given, Casselmann and Schmidt."

"That's so," said Dexter. "It was not Schmidt. Schmidt was second in command. He afterward commanded U-87, which was sunk by U.S.S. Fanning. Casselmann was the commander. Until lately he was engaged in instructional work at Kiel."

Stanford nodded.

"You knew that, too, did you? Well, he has been promoted from that job, and he is now touring Germany lecturing on behalf of the German admiralty on the value of the U-boat campaign. The Germans are trying to rouse the flagging enthusiasm of the people, and Casselmann is an orator in addition to being a bloody-minded murderer."

He said this without passion, as though he were stating some commonplace quality of the man. He opened a drawer of his desk and took out a sheet of paper.

"Here is his itinerary," he said. "He lectures at Hanover on the 17th, Magdeburg on the 19th; Cassel, which I guess is his home town, on the 21st; Frankfurt on the 24th, Heidelberg on the 27th, Nuremberg on the 29th—that was yesterday—Ingolstadt on the 31st—that's tomorrow—and Munich on the fifth."

"What do you intend doing?"

"I have sent Hooky Patterson out to get a little information," said Dexter. "Do you know the country between Ingolstadt and Augsburg? I see you don't. There's a nice wide heath between the two towns and it's fairly deserted. If Hooky does his work well, you and I will be over there on the morning of the second at 11 o'clock."

Stanford nodded and rose. As he was making for the door, Dexter stopped him.

"Stanford," he said, "it's a long time ago, but I guess you and I are feeling still too bad to put things into words. But did you ever realize the horror of being shelled in open boats?

"The maddening helplessness of it! In a little cockleshell lifeboat without any kind of cover, at the mercy of the sea, unable to move at more than two or three miles an hour, with shells fired with deadly accuracy breaking over you, do you realize what it means to sit there and watch the bullets hitting the water and sending up little fountains and waiting for the next which will burst over you?"

"For God's sake, stop!" said Stanford, hoarsely. "I was there—you forget I was there."

"Yes, you were there," Dexter seemed to be speaking to himself. "Why, of course you were there, and she was there, too."

Stanford went out and closed the door with a hand that shook.

Hooky Patterson, with a map on the holder before him, was at that moment looking for a private park. He did not want any particular private park so long as it had broad green meadows and was within easy distance of the Frankfurt-Strasbourg road, and providing it was sufficiently remote from any center of population it would fulfill his requirements. But it must be near that road which showed on his map and by the side of which was marked a long and interminable red line.

He was in a dangerous territory because the Germans maintained strong defensive squadrons between Frankfurt and Strasbourg, and in the vicinity of both those cities were large aerodromes populated by nervous and pugnacious scouts, and he was not at all anxious that he should excite their animosity.

It was late in the afternoon when he found the desirable estate. It lay back from the road and was inclosed by walls which had the appearance of being scalable.

Hooky gave a look round, shut off his engines, and dropped steeply to the park. It was as good a landing place as heart could desire. A depression in the ground gave him the cover he wanted and even from the edge of the saucer in which his airplane lay the house was out of sight.

The wall was easily climbed, and he reached the straight road on the other side. There was no fear of surprise. He had not seen a single motor car on the road for four miles. The road he crossed. Along the farther side ran the telegraph wires, supported by steel standards placed at regular intervals and running away till they were black match sticks on the level horizon.

He had a trowel in his hand, and roughly measuring with this, he first very carefully cut away the turf and laid it aside, then began to excavate at a furious speed. He had not far to dig. Two feet below the surface his trowel struck something hard and, scooping out the earth, he disclosed a small iron pipe line.

"Bong!" said Hooky, and replaced the earth, stamping it down and covering it with the slabs of turf he had cut He dusted his hands, re-climbed the wall, and gained the park. He heard the distant drone of an aeroplane and waited. His planes were camouflaged, and providing the wandering airman was flying at a reasonable height there was little chance of detection.

Soon a big German bombing plane sailed into view, glittering white in the afternoon sun, her two big black crosses clearly discernible. Hooky looked after it with a wistful eye. He judged the pilot as a veritable Hun.*

(*"Hun" in flying parlance when applied to pilots—whether they be friend or foe—means "novice.")

But an attack would bring a swarm of hornets about him. He was in the triangle Strasbourg-Metz-Munich and that was a trap from which the solitary scout might find some difficulty in escaping. His task now was to arrange some method by which he could identify the spot by night.

He started his engine, and the powerful scout pulled up the gentle slope, ran lightly along the level turf before it zoomed up at a steep angle. At 2000 feet he leveled the machine and went round in a wide circle.

There was the road—that he could see by night. Half a mile away was a little stream which would show like a ribbon of steel in the starlight. To the south was a pond.

He roughly figured the position on his map, followed the wall of the Schloss half a mile, took note of where the trees were, and jotted his observations down, then turned his nose to the west, climbing all the time, for between him and home were numerous formations, the much be-bombed Metz and the

French and American lines. He sailed serenely over Metz at a height of 20,000 feet and hardly deigned to notice the furious bombardment which greeted him.

He spent the rest of the afternoon closeted with Dexter, and at 10 o'clock that night he walked out into the darkness of the aerodrome, made a careful examination of his machine, strapped certain instruments into the fuselage and went up into the night with the share of the Great Plow and the cold brilliance of the North Star on his left front.

Metz greeted him in passing. He himself flew high to avoid bombers of both sides, who were flitting restlessly from east to west and from west to east. Bombers, however, are peaceable and well-conducted folk. It is one of the unwritten laws that bombers going about their business shall not attack other bombers going about theirs.

Hooky grinned as he witnessed a flicker of signals between opposing machines as they passed one another and spelled out the derisive and even insulting messages which they sent.

Beneath him the earth was black. Only the rivers, reflecting the starlight, showed with any clearness. The drone of his engines brought scores of wandering searchlights groping in the skies. Once they caught the tip of his wing; but before the other lights could come to hold him he had thrown over his controls, brought his right wing down, and side-slipped a thousand feet.

They did not pick him up again until he reached the environs of Strasbourg. Here quivering pencils of flame leaped at him from the darkness above and a ricochetting bullet smacked past him, hit between his feet, but fortunately missed the controls.

"Some eyesight!" said Hooky, and came round on an Immelmann turn looking for his assailant. This time he saw the flashes of the gun distinctly, fired a quick burst, and dived. The unseen scout fell behind him. He saw the blue flame of his exhaust as he dived.

For an instant Hooky hesitated. It was his instinct, and the desire for a fight urged him to put down his nose and follow. But the recollection of Dexter's parting words and the importance of his mission saved him.

"Get thee behind me, Satan!" said Hooky piously and resumed his journey.

Neither searchlight nor enemy plane had met him by the time he had reached his destination. He had dropped to two thousand feet when he located the pond and, swinging northward, picked up the stream. He dropped lower, and with difficulty found the road. Two minutes later he had dipped to the park, making his landing within 20 yards of where he had intended.

He left his engine on and his tractor ticking round slowly, took out his case of instruments, his trowel and an electric torch, and again reached the road.

He found the place where he had made his excavation, removed the turf as he had that afternoon, and scraped clear to the iron pipe line.

He laid down the small cylinder he had brought with him, fixed the pipe in the burner, and in a quarter of an hour he had cut a hole as big as a man's closed fist in the soft pipe. When he had removed the piece by means a hand vacuum and the iron had sufficiently cooled, he put in his hand and pulled out the slack of a dozen telegraph wires. They were colored red, green and yellow.

It was the yellow which interested Hooky most of all. He pulled it as far as it would come, which was about six inches, and in 10 minutes it was well and truly tapped and the tiny telegraph instrument he had brought with him, and which now rested on the ground, was clicking furiously.

He listened with the rapt joy of the artist, for Hooky Patterson's consuming vice was curiosity, and the knowledge that he was not only poking his nose into somebody else's business—for the words that beat and pulsed under his hand might be translated by the most ornamental Gothic font that printer ever set—filled him with ecstatic delight.

Kiel was talking to Great-General-Headquarters, and Great-General-Headquarters, in its lofty way, was passing instructions to Kiel. No great secrets were being revealed, if the truth be told. No disclosures of strategy, no hair-raising revelations such as you might expect would occupy the yellow line from Kiel to headquarters.

"General Statement Form N.Z. 167 is forwarded by night mail— From supply officer, Kiel, to commissariat department. Reference your wire. Experimental issue K.K. Biscuit has been favorably received. Sample 74 is forwarded this evening. Will commandant, 12th destroyer flotilla, forward discipline report due on the 17th—"

Hooky listened, entranced. Once he smothered the instrument and crouched in the grass as a big motor car flashed past, its headlights throwing two straight beams of white light and illuminating the great wall of the park. It was the only interruption.

Presently there came a lull in the conversation, and general headquarters began what was evidently a routine message with the prefix, "1263 words."

This Hooky had been waiting for. He pushed over a little lever and general headquarters talked to the grass. He dropped his hand on the sender and began urgently calling "Z.Z.Z." The reply came immediately and Hooky tapped out his message:

"Very urgent. Clear the line. Z.Z.Z. Most confidential!"

Back came the answer:

"Wait."

Hooky guessed that there was a special operator to take Z. messages and squatted patiently until the Instrument spoke again:

"Commence."

Hooky's hand dropped caressingly upon the sender.

"Most confidential. From Quartermaster General to chief of imperial naval staff. Privately instruct, by confidential officer, Lieut. Capt. H. K. Casselmann to rendezvous at 11 o'clock tomorrow morning at the crossroads between Heilbronn and Hall, at point K on squared map B. O. 173.

"He must come in car, unattended, and will be met by intelligence officer, 19th Army. Acknowledge immediately. No further telegraphic reference to these instructions must be made. Confirmation should be forwarded by letter addressed confidentially to Quartermaster General. Ends."

For a quarter of an hour Hooky waited. And all the time headquarters was babbling forth its daily routine report. At the other end of the wire the message was being digested, noted and minuted by a weary naval officer, and at the end of the quarter of an hour came the acknowledgment from Kiel.

Hooky had to wait until the long routine dispatch had exhausted itself before he reconnected the wires and sent, as from Kiel, an O.K. receipt. There might be complications. Kiel, which was in the habit of receiving the routine report, might wonder what had become of it and make inquiries. He had to possess his soul in patience for another half an hour listening to the exchange of messages, ready to jump in if any reference was made to his confidential, and it was not until 3 o'clock in the morning that he rose, cramped and stiff, put his foot upon the replaced turf, and with his instruments under his arm retraced his steps to the place where he had left his machine.

Dawn lay palely on the eastern skies when he got back to the headquarters of the Ace High, heavy-eyed but cheerful.

"I thought we had lost you, Hooky." Dexter came out of the shadowy doorway of the mess. "There's a hot meal waiting for you, son. How did you get on?"

"There's no secret in the German empire which is unknown to me, colonel," said Hooky boastfully as he stripped his leather coat, flung his helmet on to the floor, and put his frozen hands round the steaming cup of coffee which the mess waiter brought him. "I know more about the Kaiser's family life than his pet chiropodist.

"I am intimate with the guilty secrets of the Crown Prince, and I know just what's wrong with Biscuit K.K. There will probably be a new Chancellor tomorrow, or it may be the next day, and Prince Oscar has developed mumps."

"Rave on," said Dexter. "I gather you have done your work."

"As nobody else in the world could have done it," said the immodest Hooky. "I have laid the mine."

"The train is what you are trying to say. I will supply the mine. At 11 o'clock at the crossroads?"

"The lad will be there," said Hooky, "dressed to kill. He will wear a red rose in his buttonhole and carry a copy of the New York News under his left arm."

"Eleven o'clock!"

At 10 o'clock on the following morning a car passed through Karlsruhe, crossed the main Stuttgart road, reached and passed Heilbronn, and came to a wide expanse of dune and moorland south of

Osterburken. It was driven by a stoutly built young man in naval uniform who carried with him an indefinable air of importance.

Punctually to the minute of 11 o'clock he came to the crossroads. In reality it was the meeting place of seven small roads which crossed the heath, which at this hour was deserted save for two old men whom the Herr Lieutenant-Captain had passed driving a drove of pigs to Stuttgart. He pulled up sharp and looked at his watch, and as he did so a young man rose from the bushes and walked leisurely toward him.

For a moment Lieut.-Capt. Casselmann stared at the apparition.

"An enemy airman!" he gasped, and fumbled for his sword.

"Don't move, Admiral," said Hooky. "I'm not going to hurt you, but here's a letter for you."

He handed a large envelope to the bewildered officer, who looked from it to the long-barreled revolver which Hooky was swinging dexterously by the butt, humming a tune the while.

He tore open the envelope and read:

In the Spring of last year you torpedoed the "Aramac." In sinking that ship you may have obeyed the orders of your superior. In shelling the ship-wrecked passengers in open boats you obeyed merely your native lust for murder. Afloat in unprotected rowboats, surrounded by bursting shrapnel, helpless, those unhappy passengers, two of whom were nearly-related to the undersigned, experienced a terror of which you will have some taste today. You are three miles from cover. If you reach that cover, we shall not trouble you again.

It bore the signatures of Dexter and Stanford.

"What—what does it mean?"

Lieut.-Capt. Casselmann stared at the nonchalant figure of Hooky Patterson and Hooky looked up significantly. The captain followed his eyes. Poised in the blue above him was a white-winged battle plane.

Hooky took a handkerchief from his pocket and waved it twice above his head, and the machine glided down toward him. The German officer's face had gone gray. Without a word he jerked the car forward and gathering speed it flew along the road to Hall.

Hooky ran back to his scout, climbed aboard, and set her moving. He saw the car with its white trail of dust rocking at furious speed, saw the dip of the battle plane, and watched the culmination of Dexter's vendetta.

For Dexter was in the pilot's seat and the hard-faced Stanford fingered the bomb release in the observer's cockpit. The naval officer evidently knew the neighborhood. He was making for a little village where a stone church would offer him some protection.

Just before he reached a crossroad where he would turn off, the battle plane swooped ahead of him. There was a deafening crash and the air was filled with flying fragments of earth. The car swerved to the left and took the opposite road.

To pass the big hole which the bomb had made was impossible. In a flurry of fear he put over the accelerator and literally flew. If he could turn into the secondary road there was a wood through which the road passed. He was in sight of the crossways when again the battle-plane swooped and again the bomb fell true. He turned to the left again, and as he did so a bomb fell close to the side of the road, smothering him with debris and half blowing him from the seat.

He was half mad with fear. He had a horrible sense of helplessness. He was being played with as a kitten plays with a mouse. Suddenly he pulled the car to a dead stop and three of his four tires went off together.

He flung himself out, leaped a ditch by the roadside and dived into a bush. He did not hear the bomb which dropped nearby, but it lifted and flung him to the open. He staggered forward blindly.

Now a machine gun was going on him. The bullets pinged past him and raised little fountains of dust from the earth. He turned and faced his inexorable enemy and stood screaming his defiance, a tragic figure, bespattered with dust, his clothes torn, his white face moist.

"Swine! Swine! Swine!" he screamed,

A rural policeman found him three hours later wandering about the heath alternately laughing and weeping.

Dexter at that moment was pouring out a stiff whisky-and-soda and was looking into the eyes of the silent Stanford.

"We ought to have killed him," said Stanford.

"I guess not," said Dexter, with a wry face. "There, are worse things than being killed!"

Edgar Wallace – A Short Biography

Richard Horatio Edgar Wallace was born on the 1st April 1875 at 7 Ashburnham Grove, Greenwich. His mother, Mary Jane "Polly" Richards was born into an Irish Catholic family in Liverpool in 1843 and had worked in theatres, both as an actress in bit-parts and as a stagehand and usherette, until she married a Merchant Navy Captain, Joseph Richards, in 1867. He too had been born into an Irish Catholic family in Liverpool. His father had also been a Captain in the Merchant Navy, and his mother's family had a marine background. Mary was eight months pregnant with Joseph's child when he died at sea, and it was once the child had been born that she first turned to the stage, taking the stage name Polly Richards.

She joined the Marriott family theatre troupe in 1872. It was managed by Mrs. Alice Edgar, Richard Edgar, Grace Edgar, Adeline Edgar and Richard Horatio Edgar, Wallace's father. In late 1874 Mary and

Richard Horatio Edgar had a brief sexual encounter at the party following a successful show, and she fell pregnant. Worried about the scandal which would ensue and fearing that she might forever lose her job at the troupe, she fabricated an obligation in Greenwich would detain her there for at least six months. She lived in a room in the boarding house on Ashburnham Grove until her son, Edgar, was born. She had already made preparations through her midwife for a couple to foster the child, and when Edgar was born the midwife presented her with Mrs Freeman. Her husband was a fishmonger at Billingsgate market and she already had ten children. She was happy to foster the child and for Polly to make frequent visits to see him in exchange for a small sum of money which Polly made from her work in the theatre troupe.

Wallace was now known as Richard Horatio Edgar Freeman, taking his father's forenames and his foster family's surname. Broadly speaking his childhood was a happy one. The Freemans looked after him lovingly and he had good friendships with his foster siblings, particularly Clara Freeman, twenty years his senior, who often looked after him as a child. After a few years Polly's finances tightened and she was no longer in a position to afford the fee she had been paying the Freemans. However, they had grown to love the young Wallace and opted to adopt him in order to keep him out of the workhouse. Polly could no longer visit him. George Freeman was keen to ensure that he had equal opportunities and did all he could to secure him an education at St. Alfege with St. Peter's, a Peckham boarding school. Despite his adoptive father's efforts, though, Wallace left the school aged twelve for truancy.

Instead he went to work and by the time he was fourteen or fifteen he had experience selling newspapers at Ludgate Circus, near Fleet Street, as a worker in a rubber factory, as a shoe shop assistant, as a milk delivery boy and as a ship's cook. He stole from the milk company which resulted in his dismissal, and in 1894 was engaged to a local girl from Deptford named Edith Anstree, though he broke this off and instead joined the Infantry. He adopted the name Edgar Wallace which he took from Lew Wallace, the author of *Ben-Hur*, and his medical record records a diminutive 33" chest and a stunted growth. his first posting was with the West Kent Regiment in South Africa in 1896, though he did not enjoy military life, arranging to be transferred to the Royal Army Medical Corps. Though this was a less strenuous job, it was also significantly less pleasant and so he again transferred to the Press Corps, which he found suited him far better.

He was in Cape Town in 1898 where he met Rudyard Kipling and was inspired to begin writing and publishing poetry and songs. His first collection of ballads, *The Mission that Failed!* and was enough of a success that in 1899 he paid his way out of the armed forces in order to turn to writing full time. His first work was as a war correspondent for Reuters who kept him in Africa to cover the Boer War, and then for the Daily Mail in 1900 and various other periodicals after that. It was while he was in South Africa that he met and married Ivy Maude Caldecott, who was 21 when they married in 1901, despite her Wesleyan missionary father's strong opposition to the union, for several reasons, one of which was that Wallace's writing was not turning quite the profit he had expected it would. *War and Other Poems* and *Writ in Barracks,* both published in 1900, had not proved as popular as his first collection. Eleanor Clare Hellier Wallace, their first child, died of meningitis in 1903 and, in rather deep debt, they returned to London. Wallace used his contacts with the Daily Mail to get work with them in London, electing to write detective novels as a means of making quick money.

Wallace met Polly, his birth mother, in 1903. He didn't remember her from his childhood as he had been too young when she became unable to visit, so it was as though they were meeting for the first time. She was sixty years old and terminally ill, living in abject poverty. She had come to Wallace seeking financial support, but he turned her away. She died in the Bradford Infirmary later that year. In 1904 he and Ivy had a son, Bryan. He was still writing and had completed his first thriller, *The Four Just Men*. Since nobody would publish it he resorted to setting up his own publishing company which he called Tallis Press and he published a serialised version of *The Four Just Men* in 1905. He received promotional assistance from the Daily Mail in which he ran a competition for entrants to guess the method of murder in the final chapter, with a prize of £1,000 for a correct guess. Although the paper's proprietor, Lord Alfred Harmsworth, refused Wallace the £1,000 prize money, Wallace persisted and went ahead with the competition, recklessly advertising on billboards and buses all over the country, hoping to expand his advertisements across the Empire. His worried colleagues at the Daily Mail managed to convince him to lower the prize money to £500, split into a first prize of £250, a second prize of £200 and a third of £50, but with the total cost of his advertisements nearing £2,000 he would need to sell £2,500 worth of copies before he could see any profit. He was confident that this could be achieved in just three months.

Though he had remarkable enthusiasm, it became clear that his managerial skills left a lot to be desired. It soon emerged that nowhere in the competition terms and conditions had he included a clause limiting the competition to one single winner; instead, any entrant with a winning answer was entitled to their corresponding prize money. Thus, if ten entrants guessed the first prize answer, the competition was obliged to pay each entrant £250. This error was only noticed after the competition had been closed and the solution had been printed in the final installment of the novel, meaning that not only was there no opportunity to write his way out of enormous financial obligation, but the entrants who had guessed correctly would by now have read the final chapter and know they had done so. £250 was an enormous amount of money to the average Edwardian family and those entitled to it were likely to make a lot of noise if they didn't receive their money. Despite this, Wallace's fist instinct was to attempt to ignore the issue entirely, even as he discovered that he initial calculations had been dramatically over-enthusiastic and it would take nearer to two years of continuous sales to break even at the initial cost of £2,500, let alone the new figure which included every correct guesser. Compounding the problem even further was the awful realisation that as sales continued throughout the initial three month period and Wallace approached the £2,500 break-even figure, new readers were still eligible to enter and guess correctly. Though it is unknown how much he eventually owed his readers, Lord Harmsworth found himself having to loan over £5,000 in order to protect the reputation of the newspaper, since 1906 had come around and there still hadn't been a list printed of all prize-winners. It was less a charitable act than one of a man anxious that the failure would reflect ill on his own paper. Wallace filed for bankruptcy shortly thereafter and as a token gesture to his creditors sold the rights to the novel to Sir George Newnes, a publisher and editor, for £75. In the midst of this chaos though, Wallace managed to write and published *Smithy*, which would become the first of a series of *Smithy* novels.

Following this fiascos Wallace was dismissed from the Daily Mail in 1907 when inaccuracies which were found in his reporting, resulting in libel cases being brought against the paper. That year he became the first reporter to be fired from the Daily Mail and was his awful reputation prevented him from finding work at any other papers. Despite all this, though, he travelled to the Congo Free State later that year and reported on the criminal treatment of the Congolese people by King Leopold II of Belgium and the Belgian rubber companies. Up to fifteen million Congolese were killed in various atrocities, and Wallace was asked to serialise stories based on his experiences for her penny magazine *Weekly Tale-Teller*. He and Ivy had another daughter, named Patricia, in 1908. Though his new work for *Weekly Tale-Teller* was bringing in some money, their financial situation was still dire and Ivy was occasionally forced to sell off her jewellery and possessions in order to pay for food. In 1911 his Congolese stories were published in a collection called *Sanders of the River*, which quickly became a bestseller. He would publish eleven more such collections featuring a total of 102 stories of adventure and tribal life set on the river Congo.

From 1908 he started to enjoy a revival of both his success and his reputation. The majority of his initial writing he sold outright in order to make money as quickly as possible and placate his creditors in the United Kingdom and South Africa, but as his success saw the reestablishment of his reputation he began to find work once again as a journalist, beginning in horse racing for the *Week-End*, the *Evening News* and then as an editor for the *Week-End Racing Supplement*. Following this success he started his own racing papers, *Bibury's* and *R. E. Walton's Weekly*, eventually buying his own racehorses and losing thousands gambling. His success was insufficient to support his newly extravagant lifestyle and his marriage began to fail in the light of his financial irresponsibility. He and Ivy had their last child together, Michael Blair Wallace, in 1916, and she filed for divorce in 1918 moving to Tunbridge Wells with her children.

Wallace began to fall for his secretary Ethel Violet King and they married in 1921, having a child, Penelope Wallace, in 1923, who would herself go on to become a successful crime writer. Wallace now began to take his career as a fiction writer more seriously, signing with Hodder and Stoughton in 1921. He now began to organize his contracts more carefully, arranging for royalties and properly organized promotions, run by people more business-minded than himself. He was marketed as the 'King of Thrillers' and they gave him the trademark image of a trilby, a cigarette holder and a yellow Rolls Royce. He was truly prolific, capable not only of producing a 70,000 word novel in three days but of doing three novels in a row in such a manner. His publishers signed off on almost everything he wrote as soon as he turned it in, estimating that by 1928 one in four books being read at any time was written by Wallace, for alongside his famous thrillers he wrote variously in other genres, including but not limited to science fiction, non-fiction accounts of WWI which amounted to ten volumes and screen plays. Eventually he would reach the remarkable total of 170 novels, 18 stage plays and 957 short stories.

Wallace became chairman of the Press Club which to this day holds an annual Edgar Wallace Award, rewarding 'excellence in writing'. In 1923 he broadcasted a report on the Epsom Derby horse race for the British Broadcasting Company, making him the first ever radio sports correspondent. His ex-wife Ivy had suffered from breast cancer between 1923-1924, and it eventually killed her in 1926 despite a successful operation to remove a tumour the year before. He wrote the essay "The Canker in our Midst" in 1926 which dealt, aggressively and controversially, with the problem of paedophilia in show business, describing how children were unwittingly left open to sexual abuse, and linking paedophilia with homosexuality. Its tone has been described as "intolerant, blustering, kick-the-blighters-down-the-stairs". He was appointed chairman of the British Lion Film Corporation on the back of the success of *The Ringer* and on the agreement that he give British Lion first choice on all his future work. This contract gave him an annual salary and a large amount of stock with the company, along with a stipend on all British Lion production of his work and 10% of their annual profits. This extraordinary contract gave him annual earnings by 1929 of almost £50,000, or almost £2 million in 2014.

He now became an active figure in politics, entering the 1931 general election as a Liberal contestant in Blackpool, rejecting the current government in favour of free trade. He lost the election by over 33,000 votes and went to America in late 1931, once again deeply in debt after buying the *Sunday News* which closed six months later. In America he quickly found work as a script doctor for RKO Pictures, enjoying early success with the 1932 adaptation of *The Hound of the Baskervilles*. This success, along with that of the play *The Green Pack*, established his reputation in America and he was able to see his own work adapted for film, beginning with *The Four Just Men*. His most successful theatrical work, *On The Spot*, which explores the life of Al Capone, has been described as "arguably, in construction, dialogue, action, plot and resolution, still one of the finest and purest of 20th-century melodramas". These successes led to his assignation on RKO's "gorilla picture" which would become famous as King Kong in 1933.

He worked on the first draft though he was beginning to experience severe headaches which brought about a diagnosis of diabetes. Despite taking medication to address his condition, it deteriorated in a matter of days. His wife booked him passage home but soon heard that he had entered a coma and died of his condition and double pneumonia on the 7th of February 1932 in North Maple Drive, Beverly Hills. In his honour the bell at St. Bride's church on Fleet Street tolled for the duration of the morning while the flags flew at half-mast. He was buried near his home in England at Chalklands, Bourne End, in Buckinghamshire. Once again, at the time of his death he was in severe debt, mostly to racing bookkeepers, though these debts were settled within two years thanks to the enormous royalties his estate continued to receive from his contracts. His writing has been translated into 29 languages, and is considered one of the most important bodies of Colonial writing.

Edgar Wallace – A Concise Bibliography

African Novels
Sanders of the River (1911)
The People of the River (1911)
The River of Stars (1913)
Bosambo of the River (1914)
Bones (1915)
The Keepers of the King's Peace (1917)
Lieutenant Bones (1918)
Bones in London (1921)
Sandi the Kingmaker (1922)
Bones of the River (1923)
Sanders (1926)
Again Sanders (1928)

Four Just Men (Series)
The Four Just Men (1905)
The Council of Justice (1908)
The Just Men of Cordova (1917)
The Law of the Four Just Men (US title: Again the Three Just Men) (1921)
The Three Just Men (1926)
Again the Three Just Men (US title: The Law of the Three Just Men) (1929) a.k.a. Again the Three

Mr. J. G. Reeder (Series)
Room 13 (1924)
The Mind of Mr. J. G. Reeder (US title: The Murder Book of Mr. J. G. Reeder) (1925)
Terror Keep (1927)
Red Aces (1929)
The Guv'nor and Other Short Stories (US title: Mr. Reeder Returns) (1932)

Detective Sgt. (Inspector) Elk series
The Nine Bears or The Other Man or The Cheaters (1910)
revised as Silinski - Master Criminal (1930)

The Fellowship of the Frog (1925)
The Joker or The Colossus (1926)
The Twister (1928)
The India-Rubber Men (1929)
White Face (1930)

Educated Evans (1924)
More Educated Evans (1926)
Good Evans (1927)

Smithy (1905)
Smithy Abroad (1909)
Smithy and The Hun (1915)
Nobby or Smithy's Friend Nobby (1916)

Angel Esquire (1908)
The Fourth Plague or Red Hand (1913)
Grey Timothy or Pallard the Punter (1913)
The Man Who Bought London (1915)
The Melody of Death (1915)
A Debt Discharged (1916)
The Tomb of T'Sin (1916)
The Secret House (1917)
The Clue of the Twisted Candle (1918)
Down under Donovan (1918)
The Man Who Knew (1918)
The Strange Lapses of Larry Loman (1918)
The Green Rust (1919)
Kate Plus Ten (1919)
The Daffodil Mystery or The Daffodil Murder (1920)
Jack O' Judgment (1920)
The Angel of Terror or The Destroying Angel (1922)
The Crimson Circle (1922)
Mr. Justice Maxwell or Take-A-Chance Anderson (1922)
The Valley of Ghosts (1922)
Captains of Souls (1923)
The Clue of the New Pin (1923)
The Green Archer (1923)
The Missing Million (1923)
The Dark Eyes of London or The Croakers (1924)
Double Dan or Diana of Kara-Kara (US Title) (1924)
The Face in the Night or The Diamond Men or The Ragged Princess (1924)
The Sinister Man (1924)
The Three Oak Mystery (1924)
The Blue Hand or Beyond Recall (1925)

The Daughters of the Night (1925)
The Gaunt Stranger or Police Work (1925) revised as The Ringer (1926)
A King by Night (1925)
The Strange Countess (1925)
The Avenger or The Hairy Arm (1926)
The Black Abbot (1926)
The Day of Uniting (1926)
The Door with Seven Locks (1926)
The Man from Morocco or Souls In Shadows or The Black (US Title) (1926)
The Million Dollar Story (1926)
The Northing Tramp or The Tramp (1926)
Penelope of the Polyantha (1926)
The Square Emerald or The Woman (1926)
The Terrible People or The Gallows' Hand (1926)
We Shall See! or The Gaol-Breakers (US Title) (1926)
The Yellow Snake or The Black Tenth (1926)
Big Foot (1927)
The Feathered Serpent or Inspector Wade or Inspector Wade and the Feathered Serpent (1927)
Flat 2 (1927)
The Forger or The Counterfeiter (1927)
Terror Keep (1927)
The Hand of Power or The Proud Sons of Ragusa (1927)
The Man Who Was Nobody (1927)
Number Six (1927)
The Squeaker or The Sign of the Leopard or The Squealer (US Title) (1927)
The Traitor's Gate (1927)
The Double (1928)
The Flying Squad (1928)
The Gunner or Gunman's Bluff (US Title) (1928)
Four Square Jane or The Fourth Square (1929)
The Golden Hades or Stamped In Gold or The Sinister Yellow Sign (1929)
The Green Ribbon (1929)
The Calendar (1930)
The Clue of the Silver Key or The Silver Key (1930)
The Lady of Ascot (1930)
The Devil Man or Sinister Street or Silver Steel
or The Life and Death of Charles Peace (1931)
The Man at the Carlton or The Mystery of Mary Grier (1931)
The Coat of Arms or The Arranways Mystery (1931)
On the Spot: Violence and Murder in Chicago (1931)
When the Gangs Came to London or Scotland Yard's Yankee Dick
or The Gangsters Come To London (1932)
The Frightened Lady or The Case of the Frightened Lady or Criminal At Large (1933)
The Green Pack (1933)
The Man Who Changed His Name (1935)
The Mouthpiece (1935)
Smoky Cell (1935)
The Table (1936)

Sanctuary Island (1936)

Other Novels
Captain Tatham of Tatham Island or Eve's Island or The Island of Galloping Gold (1909)
The Duke in the Suburbs (1909)
Private Selby (1912)
1925 - The Story of a Fatal Peace (1915)
Those Folk of Bulboro (1918)
The Book of all Power (1921)
Flying Fifty-five (1922)
The Books of Bart (1923)
Barbara on Her Own (1926)

Poetry Collections
The Mission That Failed (1898)
War and Other Poems (1900)
Writ In Barracks (1900)

Non-Fiction
Unofficial Despatches of the Anglo-Boer War (1901)
Famous Scottish Regiments (1914)
Field Marshal Sir John French (1914)
Heroes All: Gallant Deeds of the War (1914)
The Standard History of the War – Volumes 1 – 4 (1914)
Kitchener's Army and the Territorial Forces:
The Full Story of a Great Achievement (1915)
Vol. 2-4. War of the Nations (1915)
Vol. 5-7. War of the Nations (1916)
Vol. 8-9. War of the Nations (1917)
Famous Men and Battles of the British Empire (1917)
Tam of the Scouts (1918)
The Real Shell-Man: The Story of Chetwynd of Chilwell (1919)
People or Edgar Wallace by Himself (1926)
The Trial of Patrick Herbert Mahon (1928)
My Hollywood Diary (1932)

Screenplays
King Kong (1932, first draft of original screenplay, 110 pages) While the script was not used in its entirety, much of it was retained for the final screenplay.
The Hound of the Baskervilles (1932, British film)
The Squeaker (1930, British film)
Prince Gabby (1929, British film)
Mark of the Frog (1928, American film)
The Valley of Ghosts (192

Short Story Collections
The Admirable Carfew (1914)
The Adventure of Heine (1917)

Tam O' the Scouts (1918)
The Fighting Scouts (1919)
Chick (1923)
The Black Avons (1925)
The Brigand (1927)
The Mixer (1927)
This England (1927)
The Orator (1928)
The Thief in the Night (1928)
Elegant Edward (1928)
The Lone House Mystery and Other Stories (1929)
The Governor of Chi-Foo (1929)
Again the Ringer The Ringer Returns (US Title) (1929)
The Big Four or Crooks of Society (1929)
The Black or Blackmailers I Have Foiled (1929)
The Cat-Burglar (1929)
Circumstantial Evidence (1929)
Fighting Snub Reilly (1929)
For Information Received (1929)
Forty-Eight Short Stories (1929)
Planetoid 127 and The Sweizer Pump (1929)
The Ghost of Down Hill & The Queen of Sheba's Belt (1929)
The Iron Grip (1929)
The Lady of Little Hell (1929)
The Little Green Man (1929)
The Prison-Breakers (1929)
The Reporter (1929)
Killer Kay (1930)
Mrs William Jones and Bill (1930)
Forty Eight Short Stories (George Newnes Limited ca. 1930)
The Stretelli Case and Other Mystery Stories (1930)
The Terror (1930)
The Lady Called Nita (1930)
Sergeant Sir Peter or Sergeant Dunn, C.I.D. (1932)
The Scotland Yard Book of Edgar Wallace (1932)
The Steward (1932)
Nig-Nog and other humorous stories (1934)
The Last Adventure (1934)
The Woman From the East (1934) Co-written By Robert George Curtis
The Edgar Wallace Reader of Mystery and Adventure (1943)
The Undisclosed Client (1963)

Other
King Kong, with Draycott M. Dell, (1933), 28 October 1933 Cinema Weekly

Plays
An African Millionaire (1904)
The Forest of Happy Dreams (1910)

Dolly Cutting Herself (1911)
The Manager's Dream (1914)
M'Lady (1921)
Double Dan (1926)
The Mystery of room 45 (1926)
A Perfect Gentleman (1927)
The Terror (1927)
Traitors Gate (1927)
The Lad (1928)
The Man Who Changed His Name (1928)
The Squeaker (1928)
The Calendar (1929)
Persons Unknown (1929)
The Ringer (1929)
The Mouthpiece (1930)
On the Spot (1930)
Smoky Cell (1930)
The Squeaker (1930)
To Oblige A Lady (1930)
The Case of the Frightened Lady (1931)
The Old Man (1931)
The Green Pack (1932)
The Table (1932)

www.ingramcontent.com/pod-product-compliance
Lightning Source LLC
Chambersburg PA
CBHW061455170626
46811CB00004B/1522